Feel No Evil

A NOVEL

STEPHANIE KEPKE

Cover Design by Stephanie Kepke
Proofreading by J.C. Wing
Layout by Adam Bodendieck

ISBN: 978-0-9976861-7-3
EPUB ISBN: 978-0-9976861-6-6

Don't Give Up: Written by Ryan Star, Used with Permission
Copyright: Don't Give Up, Ryan Star LTD, 2017
RAINN Used with Permission

ACKNOWLEDGMENTS

Thank you to my family, Jeff, Drew, Joshua and Aidan for your support and love. I appreciate all of you very much. Thank you to my mom, Beverly Kepke, and my siblings, Jodi Schinz; David Kepke; and Shari Morris, and their families. And thank you to all of my in-laws. Thank you to J.C. Wing for your eagle-eyed proofreading. Thank you to Adam Bodendieck for your expert layout. Thank you to Jill McCorkle for teaching me lessons that have stayed with me for decades and for your continued friendship. Your books always inspire me. Thank you to Ryan Star for allowing your amazing song, *Don't Give Up*, to be a part of this story. It fits perfectly. And thank you to Serena Lingo. Thank you to Rachel DeLadesmo and RAINN for letting me use your incredible organization in this story. A huge thank you to everyone who read this book (even just a few chapters) and everyone who chimed in on the many versions of the cover I designed (many did both): Melissa Levine; Shari Goldberg; Liz Danziger; Scott Syat; Joy Weiser; Lucia Reichard; Galit Segal; Cheryl Popiel; Aliza Greenberg; John Giannone; Kathy Barstow; Randy Brown; Steve Osterweil; Heather Peretz; Amy Olsen; Judy Karul; Adam Weinstock; Jeannie Feldman; Beth Tabak; Jennifer Federmann; Dr. Victoria Frisse; Beth Meyer; Sharon Balkman; Kaycee John; Teresa Medina; Beth Foley; Julie Sebell; Lisa Scuderi-Burkimsher; Lisa Hindi; Donna Sansaricq; Nina Gilbert; Leslie Kniffin;

Michele Santoro; Gina Lewis; Deb Baer; Lisa Zimmerman; Stephanie Horn; Tracy Gorman and Kerrie Irish. I'm so sorry if I've missed anyone—I still appreciate you!

Thank you to my early Kickstarter supporters (before this book went to production): Lisa Scuderi-Burkimsher; Rachel Strehlow; Caryn Wolin; Patricia Raifer; Vivian Chen; Kathy Barstow; Randy Brown and Shari Morris.

Most importantly, thank you to everyone—friends, family, readers—who have supported my writing and encouraged me. It means the world to me.

For Survivors Everywhere:
May you rise up and be heard.

AUTHOR'S NOTE

This book started as a short story a decade ago, but readers wanted more. At first, it was an arduous task to turn it into a novel—I didn't see a clear journey for Kate, and the subject matter was dark and close to the bone. I set it aside, and finished a novel, *Goddess of Suburbia* (and a film script adaptation of the novel); a book of essays, *Boys, Dogs and Chaos* (and a one-woman show based on those essays); and had two novellas published, as well—*A New Life* and *You & Me*. When the #MeToo movement exploded, along with rise of political divisiveness in our country, Kate's story suddenly became crystal clear. It was then that I reached out to RAINN (Rape, Abuse & Incest National Network) and requested to use their organization in a pivotal scene. This added to the narrative, of course, but that wasn't the most important thing. The most important thing to me was to raise awareness of how survivors of sexual assault can get the help they need. If you are a survivor, call 800.656.HOPE (4673) or visit https://www.rainn.org/. They can help.

If you're battling an eating disorder, there's hope and help for you, as well. Visit https://www.nationaleatingdisorders.org/help-support/contact-helpline, even if all seems hopeless. You can call, chat or text.

You can also reach out to me on my Facebook page: https://www.facebook.com/stephaniekepkewriter. If you need someone to listen, send me a direct message. You'll get an auto reply first, but I will respond. Although many readers have reached out to me about my essays on eating disorders, I've never included this in an author's note. But, here's the thing…I hope this is more than just a book—I hope it makes a difference. If this book sets even one reader on the path to healing; if it makes even one reader feel less alone, all of my hard work will be worth it. Thank you for reading.

PART ONE

CHAPTER ONE

April 2014

2:21. 2:22. 2:23. ALL I COULD see were the digital numbers of the clock. All I could hear was his menacing voice, "Is it going to be hard or soft?" All I could say was, "Please stop. Please don't." See no evil. Hear no evil. Speak no evil. They forgot feel no evil. All I could feel were his hands pushing down on my shoulders and the searing pain ripping through my core.

I close the journal—the flowers on its cover faded; the paper almost silk-like from age. It has been over twenty years—twenty-one years, to be exact—since I wrote those words. I wish that they were fiction from a long ago college creative writing class, but they aren't—they're real, and every year on the anniversary of my assault I pull out that journal and read that entry. After I read it, I put the journal back in my old leather briefcase on top of my closet and drink a glass of wine. It's my way of marking the anniversary and moving forward. My husband, Caleb, keeps our kids downstairs or even takes them out for a slice of pizza or ice cream, so I can read it alone, in peace. So I can shed a tear or two.

I know that it might seem odd for a forty-one year old woman to still think about something that happened so long ago, but if you've ever been assaulted, you know that the fact of what happened never really goes away. It just sits like a rotten little bit of food in the back of the refrigerator. The smell will eventually take over the whole thing if you ignore it, so every year I pay attention to it—I take out that rotten bit of food, throw it in the symbolic garbage and try not to think about it, until it starts festering again a year later. It's an odd ritual, to be sure, but one that works for me or at least it did work, until this year.

It's a cruel joke being raped on Tax Day—for at least a few months before commercials always reminded me that the day is coming. "Don't forget, April fifteenth is right around the corner," a voice would ominously intone. It was always everywhere, warning people of the day of doom. It's not as much anymore with extensions and early filing, but for me it's still the lead up to reading that passage. I know I'll pull down the briefcase; I know I'll open it to the same page; and I know that I'll put it back and lock down any thoughts of that April fifteenth so many years ago for another twelve months. But as I put back the briefcase, I know that this year is different. This year I might not be able to lock it down. This year, the person who destroyed my life, Vin Merdone, just popped up on Facebook as "someone I might know" three days before April fifteenth, and I realized that while he damn near ruined my life, his life just went on as happy as could be.

With morbid curiosity I had clicked through his profile pictures. There were pictures of him smiling on a beach; swimming with dolphins; lazing on a lounge; emerging from a pool; and one that looked to be from several years earlier of him holding up a beer, no doubt saying "cheers" to the person taking the picture. He looked happy and tan—and, quite honestly, had a slight menace about him, muscles bulging beneath the tattoos covering his arms—in all of them. The worst photo by far was the one of him kneeling next to a large shark lying in a pool of blood. The smile on his face was broad and satisfied, a cruel glint in his eye. I quickly moved on, the knot in my stomach tightening. One glance at his *About* told me that he now makes Miami his home. It didn't look like he had a wife and kids, thankfully, but it did look like he was living a dream life—wealth and luxury abounded in all the photos, leaving me envious and angry in equal measure.

And the shock of seeing his face after all these years cut right through me—sure, he was older, but the set of his jaw remained, the curl of his lip was the same. He still had a full head of hair—slicked back in most photos, giving him a look of smarmy intensity. When I clicked on our mutual friend, shock morphed into anger. The thought that my old friend, Sean, the friend who introduced us that fateful night, the friend who apologized so profusely and swore up and down that he didn't know Vin was violent, the friend I thought I loved was still friends with this person, even on Facebook, filled me with a feeling I couldn't quite name—rage, surprise, despair. Or perhaps it was all of those rolled into one.

I quickly "unfriended" Sean and started to block Vin. Only I couldn't. It was like passing a car crash on the highway—I just had to look at it. I had to try to make sense of the man he is now, so maybe I could understand the boy he was then. Staring at his grinning face, I once again berated myself for only filing an anonymous police report—one that went on his record but didn't get him arrested.

Even worse, looking at those pictures, I spun back to that night. I had been drinking—I always admitted that, but I would never agree that drinking made me a victim, that anything other than violence made me a victim. Sean was hosting a party in his dorm room, and Vin was there. After we talked for most of the party, Vin asked me to take a walk. Up until that point in my life, my sophomore year in college, I had only encountered people with good intentions. Even the drunk guys who hit on me at parties, took a "no" in stride and moved on to the next girl. If I did go home with someone, they too took my "no" in stride and were content to just fool around a bit before I went back to my dorm room. I had never slept with anyone at college, and I was proud of my ability to stand my ground. That all changed on an early spring night when I was twenty years old.

Vin was charming, regaling me with stories of growing up in the city, a hardscrabble kid who spent every day after high school training at a run-down boxing gym, but still worked his way into a scholarship to our small, liberal arts college in the country. He wanted to be a journalist, a music writer, and promised to take me to see his favorite band the next time they played in town. I liked the juxtaposition of tough guy and creative soul, so when he asked me to take a walk with him to look at the stars an easy "sure" slipped from my lips. Why wouldn't I?

As soon as we stepped outside, he asked if I minded making a stop at his dorm. The spring night had turned chilly and he wanted to get a sweatshirt. For days, weeks, even months after, I beat myself up over the fact that I didn't just stay in the lobby. When he said, "Do you want to come up?" I should have said, "No, I'll wait here."

I should have run back to my dorm, but I didn't. I went up to his room and my life was never the same. As soon as we stepped in, he closed the door and locked it. He pushed me on the bed and climbed on top of me. It was so sudden and so shocking that I didn't even know what to say, "Uh, uh, uh," I spluttered. Then I managed to roll out from under him and bolt toward the door.

He stopped me, putting his arm up over my head, holding the door shut as I tried to pull it. He turned me toward the full-length mirror behind the door and ran his hand down the side of my face, "So beautiful," he whispered. "And I bet you're a real firecracker in bed—they say redheads are wild. So, why are you fighting me?"

"Let me go," I hissed. Then I screamed. My screams brought feet running towards the door, followed by banging on it and a loud and deep, "Open up!" As I tried to yell for help, Vin covered my mouth and only a muffled whimper came out.

"Go away," Vin barked at the person, and he did. To this day I wonder who that person was—who listened to that "Go away" and decided that it was more important than my screams. It didn't matter of course. No one else bothered to try to save me—not even when Vin dragged me out to the bathroom a few minutes later, growling, "I need to take a piss, and you have to come with me. I don't trust you to stay if I leave you here alone." Of course, he was right. I would have left in a second.

Our dorms had co-ed bathrooms, so no one thought twice about a guy and a girl heading into the bathroom together. Even though there were tears streaming down my face, even though his hand gripped the top of my arm as he dragged me. I stood in that stall while Vin urinated, my face to the metal wall, trying desperately to think of a way to escape. If I went under the stall would he turn, showering me with urine and pull me back by my leg? Would he catch me and smash my face into the wall? I didn't know.

There was nothing I could do but stand there. Of course, after, I went through all of the possible scenarios in my head obsessively. If I had just slid under the stall and run out, someone surely would have helped me. If I had screamed loudly enough, maybe someone would have come to my rescue. But that night I was paralyzed. I was a twenty-year-old girl, and I just didn't see a way out.

Back in Vin's room, he pushed me back on that bed with black satin sheets that rose up in my dreams afterward like they had a life of their own. He held me down so hard that the next day I was left with purple fingerprints ringing both of my shoulders. I remember going to my favorite teacher, my creative writing professor, two days later not saying a word, just pulling my shirt back to show her my shoulders, and she knew right away. She sent me to the Women's Counseling Center on campus, and I told my story.

My counselor marveled that I never cried. "How are you so strong?" she asked every time I came to see her. "What you've been through is so horrendous, Kate, even the strongest person would cry. I think you really need to cry," she implored, so I never went back.

I called my high school boyfriend with whom I had broken up just a few months before, but remained close, and told him what had happened. I heard a loud thud and he said, "Sorry, Kate, I just punched a hole through the wall. I'll need to call you back." The next weekend he drove five hours to my school from his. When he arrived, he asked around and found out where Vin lived. He put Vin's head through a wall rather than just his fist.

Violence begat more violence as little by little people heard about what happened. A friend who had a crush on me and lived on the floor below Vin called me up a few days after and said, "Hey, Kate, I'm smoking a victory joint. Just beat the crap out of Vin. So, will you go out with me now?"

"You don't get it," I whispered. No one got it. My roommate, Heather, told me not to press charges because I would just get blamed since I had been drinking. "Let the boys keep beating him up," she said between cracks of gum.

"That's vigilante justice, the best kind. Like Steven Seagal. He's so hot."

I didn't care about vigilante justice. I didn't care about much of anything. I dyed my fiery copper locks the muddiest brown I could find on the drugstore shelves. It took a year to grow it out, and even then, I had to cut it to shoulder length from halfway down my back just to get what was left off. My mom was furious with me, but I couldn't explain why I did it. In the weeks after the attack, I still took the hottest showers I could stand, trying to wash traces of Vin off of me, even after they were long gone. I wandered around campus, hollow eyed, lack of sleep threatening to derail my studies and my sanity. I couldn't go back to the Women's Center because I didn't cry in front of people, and I wasn't about to start. I couldn't talk to my friends because they didn't understand.

The only person who seemed to listen to me was Sean, even though he was the one who had introduced me to Vin. I had stumbled back to his room that night, and he held me all night long as I trembled and bit my lip, holding back tears. He didn't try to beat up Vin. He just listened to me, no doubt feeling guilty about introducing us.

It was Sean's idea to file the anonymous police report. He reasoned that if Vin did it to anyone else, that report would show up and he'd get kicked out of school for sure. He went with me to the campus police station and held my hand while I waited to fill out paperwork. That night, I slept on the couch in his dorm room. He tucked me in with a soft blanket and kissed my forehead. In fact, most nights I slept on the couch in his dorm room under that soft blanket. It was the only place I felt safe.

Slowly, I fell in love with Sean, because he was the only person who didn't answer violence with violence, who didn't judge me. But we didn't date. I was terrified of losing him if things went sour, and I wasn't ready to date anyway. Heather couldn't understand why I didn't tell Sean how I felt. "He's the one I go to when anything goes wrong," I explained.

"That's the person you're supposed be with," she insisted. "Your boyfriend *should* be the person you go to for everything. I just don't understand why you're so stubborn." She shook her head.

It was simple to me—if I dated Sean, and we had a fight, to whom would I run? No one, because there was no one else who could comfort me like he did. Yes, I still suffered from night terrors, even when he held me. I was still afraid to walk anywhere alone. But when we were together, I somehow felt safe—or at least safer than anywhere else.

But even Sean had his limits. Even Sean couldn't sit by and watch me suffer endlessly without trying to fix me. I wanted him to just listen to me when I called in the middle of the night or showed up at his door, but he begged me to get help. I told him I didn't need it. "I'm strong," I insisted, after waking on his couch at the crack of dawn, shaking. A year after the assault I still slept on Sean's couch in his apartment some nights, and he still woke whenever I did, just to comfort me.

"Getting help doesn't mean you're not strong, Kate," Sean whispered right before he kissed me for the first and last time. "It just means you're smart." The kiss was crackling with the electricity between us and gentle at the same time. It was everything I dreamed it would be, and it filled me with terror. I threw on my sweatshirt and left.

Walking home in the stillness of early morning, I knew it was the wrong decision, but I couldn't go back. I couldn't risk losing Sean if I wasn't ready to be with someone—and I truly didn't know if I was ready. It was easier to not even try. And I definitely wasn't ready to hear that I needed help. Even just considering it made me see myself as weak. I called Sean when I got back to the off-campus house I lived in with Heather and three other girls. "I'm sorry I left," I whispered.

"No, I'm sorry. I shouldn't have kissed you."

"I didn't leave because of the kiss. It had nothing to do with it."

"What was it then?"

"Look, you've been there for me during one of the toughest times of my life, and if there's anyone I'd want to be with, it's you. But I'm afraid I won't be ready to do more, and I don't want to risk losing you. I just..." I paused, searching for the right words. "I just can't be with you like that right now."

"I would never push you, Kate. I respect you so much. It was just a kiss. I didn't expect it to lead to anything else. I think you know me well enough by now to know that."

"I know," I said quietly. "I'm just scared of losing you— what if we get together, and it's not good for you. I haven't been with anyone at all since what happened with Vin." His name was poison in my mouth. It lingered on my tongue. I grabbed a bottle of juice out of the mini-fridge I kept in my room and quickly took a swig, swishing it around my mouth. "If we were ever together..." Sean began before pausing, his voice low and unmistakably sexy. "It would be amazing. Really, *really* amazing. I just know it. That one kiss..." He trailed off.

"You know, Heather said that if we ever slept together, it would be like finding the lost planet," I confided.

"Smart girl, that Heather. It would be."

I knew Sean was right. But I just couldn't let go of the pain and fear. Or perhaps I just wasn't ready to—it was safer to stay surrounded by an impenetrable wall and blame it on the *incident*, as I often called it. And Sean kept his word—he didn't push me at all. In fact, he never even tried to kiss me again. We simply settled back into our friendship—easy banter, dinners that never turned into breakfasts. I hardly even slept over at Sean's apartment anymore. Just once in a while I crashed on his couch after a night out and left before he woke. He dated a lot of girls our senior year—a different one every weekend—perhaps to fill the void left by the evaporation of our potential. We remained very close, but as the last of our college days slowly became memories, it was clear that I had missed my chance.

Still, I missed Sean terribly when I moved home after graduation. I didn't know how I would handle life without him as my safety net, so by the fall I moved back to our college town where he had stayed to get his master's in forensic psychology. I almost told him that I loved him when he shared that he wanted to pursue that field so that he could put people like Vin behind bars. Almost. I wanted the moment to be perfect. I wanted to be ready to give everything of myself to him, and I still wasn't ready to have sex with anyone. Not even Sean.

As crazy as it may seem to move away from home for just a friend, I wanted to be close to him. And not just because we hung out most weekends, curled up on his couch, watching movies. Not even because he listened to me if I called in a panic at 2:30 am, shaking from the nightmares that still haunted me. No, I wanted to be in the same town because I wanted to be able to act the moment I was ready.

I had it all planned out—I would bring over a bottle of our favorite wine, maybe some Chinese food and *When Harry Met Sally* to watch on video. While we were on the couch watching the movie, I'd tell Sean that he was my Harry, and then kiss his neck, moving my way down. I'd slowly unzip his jeans and take him in my mouth just to show him that I was okay with it after everything that happened. I imagined him carrying me to his room and making love to me so gently that all the pain locked up inside of me would just release in a torrent of tears. The good kind. I wouldn't be broken anymore because Sean's love would fix me.

Only, I waited too long for that perfect moment, not realizing that there's no such thing. A moment is perfect when you make it that way—it doesn't just magically present itself. I finally understood that when Sean called me before dawn one morning to tell me that he'd gone on a date with a woman from one of his classes, Nicole. "It was amazing," he whispered. "We connected instantly and talked all night. I just left. She's unlike anyone I've dated, maybe because she's older—twenty-seven. She knows what she wants and is strong and smart. I'm so sorry I woke you, but I just had to tell you." I cried myself back to sleep.

None of the women he dated before mattered to him, so they didn't matter to me. But this one…this one mattered. It was a punch to the gut to realize that Sean wasn't "mine" anymore—if he ever was. The more serious Sean got with Nicole, the further apart we grew. He admitted to me early on that Nicole was a little jealous of our relationship, and until he knew exactly where they were going, we wouldn't be able to hang out as much. "It's not that I'm choosing her over you, it's just that she's my girlfriend, and it's still kind of new. I need to respect her wishes. You understand, right?"

I had no choice. "Sure, I understand. You do what you need to do—I'll be here." That was when I stopped eating. I shouldn't say that—I ate, but only the simplest food possible. My guts were shredded with pain at all times—the cost of being strong and not crying, I know that now—and nothing sat well in me. My diet shrank to a few choices that didn't leave me doubled over in pain and guzzling Pepto Bismol— plain English muffins, toast, pasta and baked potatoes. And even those I ate in small amounts. It wasn't the first time food became the enemy, and it wouldn't be the last, but it was the hardest to claw my way back from.

I lost almost twenty pounds, and my once womanly curves diminished into boyish angles. At 5'2" I weighed eighty-six pounds. Deep down I knew I needed help, but I couldn't admit it. And there was only one person I wanted next to me. Only one person whom I felt I could trust. I dated here and there, but never for more than a month or two and usually just weeks—as soon as sex was on the table, I was gone. Sean was the only man I trusted enough to even consider it. After we drifted apart, I called him one night and asked him to meet me at our favorite haunt. He was also the one person I felt I could talk to about what I had become. And because, well, I missed him. I hadn't seen him in several months, and we rarely talked on the phone. His hand flew over his mouth when I walked into the bar. "What did you do to yourself?" he blurted out.

"What do you mean?" I looked down at myself, smoothed out my miniskirt; adjusted the straps on my tank top. Of course, I couldn't see just how bad my jutting collar bones, my knobby knees and my skeletal arms really were.

Sean struggled for words, "It's just, well. I don't know—you used to be so hot, so…curvy."

"I don't ever want to see you again," I spat. I turned and bolted out the door, tears streaming down my face. Of course, Sean followed me out, grabbed my elbow and turned me around.

"I'm so sorry," he whispered. "I'm just worried about you. It looks like you're killing yourself, and I'll say it again, I think you need help. I shouldn't have said anything about being 'hot.' It was just—I haven't seen you in months and it surprised me. It slipped out—that's all. Of course, you still look good. You'll always look good to me. You know, I miss you, Kate." He grinned, his soulful, dark chocolate eyes crinkling, his spiked up tawny blonde hair looking almost like a halo under the streetlight, and my heart tumbled a little bit. I wanted to pull him to me. I wanted to kiss him, melt into him. Even more, I still craved his support, and I still missed him, too. But I didn't want to get help. I didn't think I needed help.

"I miss you, too, but you have a girlfriend now. We'll never know what could've happened between us." I bit my lip and turned away. I didn't want him to see me cry.

"I'm so sorry, Kate, but I couldn't wait around forever for you. You knew how I felt about you, and yet you made it clear I was just a friend."

"Do you think I would have moved four hours away from my home and my family for just a friend, Sean?" At that point I didn't even care that the tears were streaming down my face. "Do you?"

"No, I guess not. But why didn't you tell me? Why didn't you ever say how you felt?"

"I was going to—I was going to bring a bottle of wine and *When Harry Met Sally* over and blow you."

"Well, that's just not fair to tell me that now…" Sean looked away, and I couldn't tell if he was serious or joking around. "Why would you tell me that now when there's not a fucking thing I can do about it?" I got my answer in the anger and frustration lacing his voice.

"It's not too late. Maybe we *are* meant to be. Maybe Nicole was just a place holder, so I could get my head together, and we could try." I felt a little guilty trying to break them up—I was just proving that Nicole was right to be jealous of me. But my love for Sean was stronger than the guilt.

"It *is* too late, Kate. I got engaged last week. I didn't know how to tell you—I was glad when you called, so I could tell you in person. Things have just been in a whirlwind, and I didn't get to call you, though I wanted to. I really did."

"But you didn't, Sean. You didn't bother to tell me. We were best friends for so long. I moved here to be closer to you—so as soon as I was ready for a relationship, you'd be right there."

"You weren't ready for a relationship, though, and I didn't know if you'd ever be. I also didn't know if your being not ready was an excuse, and you just didn't see me that way."

"You know I loved you."

"How could I have known, Kate?" Sean just stared at me, and I didn't know what to say. "That's what I thought, I couldn't know. Right?"

"Right," I said quietly.

"Look, I'm sorry. I'm sorry we drifted apart. I'm sorry I didn't tell you I got engaged, and I'm sorry that you've been having such a hard time and I didn't know."

"How'd we drift so far apart that I didn't even know you got engaged, Sean? How did that happen?" I asked angrily, not giving him a chance to answer. "I'll tell you how—Nicole didn't want you to see me, and you listened. Our friendship didn't mean anything to you. Goodbye, Sean. Congratulations on your engagement." I climbed into my car and drove away.

I never called Sean again. Part of me blamed him. I felt that if he truly cared about me, he would have waited patiently for me to be ready to give myself to him. He would have pushed me harder to get the help I needed so we could be together. If he truly cared about me and missed me, he would have tried harder to stay in my life instead of letting Nicole banish me. But the more rational part of me realized that no matter how hard he pushed, until I was ready to get help, it wouldn't have mattered. And honestly how long could I have expected him to wait for me?

Over the years I kept up with Sean's life through our mutual friends. I still cared about him, how could I not? I heard about when he and Nicole married a year after we last spoke. And when his first child was born, I almost sent a card, but didn't. I still missed his friendship, and I knew that he had been right all along. I had needed help.

A few months after the last time I saw Sean, I was driving down a long, dark road on my way back from visiting my family for the weekend when "I Haven't Got Time for the

Pain" came on the radio. I was exhausted, emotionally and physically, and still had an hour of driving ahead of me. At dinner that night I had eaten only a roll and a few bites of plain pasta, ignoring the looks from everyone at the table. After dinner, my mother pleaded with me to move home so she and my family could take care of me. I told her I was fine. I told her that life on my own was just great. But as my high beams danced with the moonlight on that long drive, I listened to Carly Simon croon, and knew I wasn't fine. "I'm done," I whispered. "No more."

The next day I pulled a creased business card from my wallet and dialed the number I knew by heart. My doctor had recommended a therapist who specialized in eating disorders. I balked, protesting that I didn't have an eating disorder. He pressed the card into my hand and said softly, "Yes, you do. You just don't realize it, and that's the most dangerous combination. If you don't get help, you're going to wind up hospitalized, because I'm going to put you there." I decided the doctor couldn't put me in the hospital if I didn't go back to him. Simple enough. I was in no rush to get help. I looked at the card for weeks. I moved it from my night table to my desk to my wallet. I memorized the number. I even called once or twice but hung up.

Making that call was the hardest thing I had ever done, because it meant admitting out loud that I needed help. But I made it, and I began seeing Robin, a soft-spoken social worker who managed to get me to shed a tear here and there. More importantly, she got me to realize that there was something a lot deeper behind my stomach ills, more than just an intolerance to all but the plainest food. My fear of getting back into life and relationships was deeply entwined with a fear of food.

Little by little, I faced the fears left so deeply entrenched in me by the rape. And little by little, I started to eat more. By the time I met my husband a year later, I had gained over ten pounds and some of my curves back. I ate butter on my bread and marinara sauce on my pasta. I ate chicken and vegetables and pizza. I smeared cream cheese on my bagels. I was getting, if not happy, then at least content. My anxiety, unhappiness and fear no longer defined me. I teetered on the brink of normalcy.

Of course, I told my husband, Caleb, about what had happened to me, but at that point it wasn't the center of my story anymore. The rest of my life took up the middle—my job that had morphed from entry level telemarketing into actual research and development for a marketing and events firm, my work volunteering at the local animal shelter, my new apartment. Even though what spurred me to live on my own hours from my family—my friendship with Sean—was gone, I stayed in our little college town, making a life here.

I loved stopping at the coffee shop in the morning and browsing in the bookstore in the evening. I loved the energy and charm of the town, and those were all the things I shared with Caleb. I had met him at the coffee shop one afternoon when he was in town on business. He worked in Boston and lived there, too, but that day he was at a conference at the college. He caught my eye as soon as I walked in the door of Percolating Paradise. He was sitting alone at a small table writing in a spiral notebook. He looked so serious in his horn-rimmed glasses and impeccable navy pinstripe suit. He even sported a pocket square that matched his tie, but not exactly. It complimented it—both had shades of Kelly green and navy, but the tie was a windowpane plaid and the pocket square was gingham. His thick mahogany hair fell in a side-parted wave over his forehead in that early 2000s style, the sun streaming through the window next to his table sparking it with bits of copper.

When he glanced up at me his eyes literally took my breath away. They were light green in the sun, like sea glass, set off by the green in his tie and pocket square and perfectly framed by his green-flecked tortoise shell glasses. There was an intelligence in them, too, that stopped me in my tracks. Caleb seemed like someone I could talk to about things that mattered. I got all that in just a glance.

I ordered my coffee and scone, trying not to glance back at him and seem too desperate to meet him. But when I turned around after paying, he smiled at me, and I was done. He pulled me right in with that warm and welcoming smile. It was more than just his physical appearance, though…there was just something in his demeanor that seemed different from anyone I had met since moving back to Rolling Green. My armor hadn't cracked in a very long time, but when he asked, "Would you like to join me?" and stood up to pull out the seat across from him, a bit of daylight reached my guarded heart.

At that point, the assault was just around the fuzzy edges—always there, but not in sharp focus. Honestly, if I had met Caleb a year earlier when that night was still front and center, I don't know how long we would have lasted. Caleb is kind and thoughtful, and I truly love him, but I found out pretty quickly that he likes things easy and happy. When we started dating, he told me that he loved that I was so low maintenance—I've spent a good number of years painting the picture that I am, even if deep inside, I'm not. I practice tai chi and meditate. I try not to scream, even when I want to. I work hard to make sure that the sinister thread of darkness woven through the fabric of my existence never wraps itself around my brain again.

Of course even as my adult life unspooled with relatively little drama—married a great guy, had two babies, Jacob and Oliver—there were times that the scars of being assaulted sprang to the surface in moments I would never have expected. One morning just before dawn when Jacob was a toddler, he climbed on top of me to get into my bed, pushing down on my shoulders. I screamed and bolted upright, nearly tossing him off the bed. The primal fear that enveloped me was a shock; I thought I was over it. Jacob started screaming, too, and Caleb shot up as well, yelling, "What's wrong? What's wrong?" I told him I thought I saw a spider—a ridiculous lie—I just couldn't admit the truth.

But as the years went by and our kids got bigger and our lives more hectic, I was able to compartmentalize that fear into a very back corner of my brain—one I only unlocked once a year on that anniversary. And that worked—it really did, until Vin showed up on Facebook. I had reconnected with Sean a few years earlier on Facebook. I missed his friendship, and when he popped up as someone I might know, I saw it as an opportunity to apologize for the last time we saw each other; I saw it as a chance to make amends.

Before sending him a friend request, I scrolled slowly through his pictures. I saw that he had four kids, and I felt a twinge of jealousy—I always wanted four kids, but Caleb insisted we stop at two. For years I argued for another, and I even tried to get "accidentally" pregnant, which I did eventually—I wasn't proud of it, but Caleb was actually excited when he found out that I was expecting.

It wasn't as nefarious as it sounded. I didn't skip taking my pill or poke a hole in my diaphragm. We used the rhythm method, and I told Caleb that it was a safe time when I wasn't quite sure if it was. I figured if he was willing to use the rhythm method, he should be able to handle a surprise pregnancy. And he was able to handle it—he even admitted that he too was kind of hoping I would get accidentally pregnant, but making a conscious decision to have another child filled him with fear. I think I knew that, which is why I said it was safe when it wasn't. What could have destroyed us though, made us stronger. We were both over the moon, but I had a miscarriage at eleven weeks, and even though we tried in earnest after I lost the baby, I couldn't get pregnant again.

By the time I saw Sean's pictures I had given up my dream of having a bigger family—things had just gotten too easy with the four of us, but for just a moment I found myself imagining another reality in which there was never a Nicole. A reality in which I told Sean my true feelings, and we married and had babies—a lot of babies—young. An alternate reality in which I said, "You know what—you're right; I need help, and I want you there with me while I get better. I love you, and I want to be with you, even though I freaked out over a little kiss."

Or even an alternate reality in which he said, "No, don't walk away. I love you. I want a chance to see what we could be together. I want to stay by your side while you get strong." I didn't know if my little fantasy was simply the result of my envy over his brood or unresolved feelings for Sean, so I didn't contact him right away.

After a few days, I decided that contacting him was harmless—who hasn't fantasized about an alternative path to their lives? Kind of like those *Choose Your Own Adventure* books I loved when I was a kid. I sent Sean a friend request with a message saying that it had been years, but that I hoped he forgave me for the way I acted the last time I saw him. I told him that I did eventually get help and that I was happy. I didn't tell him that sometimes I wondered what could have been if he had waited for me. Those thoughts belonged in the past.

I heard back from him right away. He said that of course he forgave me and that he was happy that my life had turned out so great. And, while we didn't talk often on Facebook, we did post birthday wishes on each other's wall and send each other the occasional *How are you doing?* message. Nothing I could feel guilty about, and just knowing that I could "talk" to him, even on Facebook, made me feel, well, happy.

But…when I saw that he was Facebook friends with Vin, I lost any sense of warmth that I may have had for him. In fact, I was furious. When he wrote to me a week later to ask why I unfriended him, explaining that he was going to send me a message and saw that we were no longer friends, I didn't even ask him about the message he was going to send. I just didn't care.

I simply answered with a missive about loyalty and sensitivity and honoring our friendship, which obviously meant nothing to him. I said that I couldn't believe that after everything that Vin had put me through, after the ramifications of that night that lasted far longer than I could have imagined—that he would accept a friend request from him, or even worse, send him a friend request himself. I told him that even as an adult I still had moments of fear that I would slip back into an eating disorder if something sparked my memories deeply enough. That was the root of why seeing Vin on Facebook terrified me. I knew that it's such a gossamer line between well and unwell, between balanced and on the edge, ready to tumble over the precipice.

I was terrified that seeing him would send me careening back to those days when food was my enemy and just getting through the day was a monumental task. And I couldn't believe that Sean would be the one to put me in that position. Vin wouldn't have shown up if we didn't have a friend in common. I would have been blissfully unaware that he was out there in cyberspace, collecting friends and showing off pictures of his beach house and extravagant lifestyle. I would have assumed that he was rotting in jail somewhere. I would have assumed that someone, far braver than I, reported him for another heinous crime, and he paid the price. But no, now I had irrefutable evidence that he hadn't paid any price at all—that he may have even done what he did to me to others and probably never had to face the consequences. And I felt that my knowing all this was Sean's fault. I hated him for letting Vin off the hook, for not saying, "You ruined my friend's life, I loved her, and you ruined her. You ruined the possibility of us."

I blamed Vin for the wall around me that kept Sean out so long ago. I blamed him for the shock on Sean's face when he saw me at the bar after all those months. I learned in therapy that Vin caused the eating disorder. Vin ruined mine and Sean's chance at happiness. He ruined what could have been. I think it would have been easier if Sean and I had dated—if we had a romantic relationship, instead of just a friendship, and it simply ran its course. Regret is the most insidious of emotions.

I was so mad that all of those feeling had to be stirred up again. I was so mad that my tidy little life with my husband and my two wonderful boys suddenly felt like a house of cards about to tumble. Sean wrote back to me right away that he was sorry and that he would be happy to unfriend him if that would make me feel better; of course, he never liked him. He was just being polite in accepting Vin's friend request. I didn't write back.

Now as I slip that time-worn flowered journal back into my leather briefcase and lift it up onto the top shelf of my closet, I wonder if I should write back to him. I don't feel like having a glass of wine, but I brought one up with me, so I sit down in my reading chair and lift it to my lips. It burns slightly as it goes down, and I make a mental note not to buy this white anymore. I always drink white wine after reading the journal. Red would seem like blood, and it gives me a headache anyway.

I take a few more sips and grab my laptop off of my bed. I click on Facebook and then Sean's messages to me. I stare at his face in the little thumbnail and wonder how we managed to hurt each other so much. One of Sean's roommates told me that Sean was devastated when I ran away from our one kiss. I thought that he must have been exaggerating—after all, it was only a kiss. Now I wonder if he really was devastated.

Maybe he thought that I didn't care about him enough to try to get better, to try to let him in.

It wasn't that I didn't care. I cared too much. Sean saw me as I was, and it scared the hell out of me—plain and simple. As long as I was alone, I couldn't bring anyone down with me, I reasoned back then. Looking back on it, I finally understand that it was just as hard for him to watch me suffer, and maybe that was why he didn't try harder to convince me to give us a chance. It's awful watching someone you love destroy herself. And I do believe he loved me.

After I went to therapy, after I started eating, I thought about contacting Sean and telling him I was better. I knew he was engaged to Nicole, but some small selfish part of me desperately wanted one more chance. I imagined him realizing the marriage would be a mistake, realizing that he was meant to be with me. I just couldn't do it. It wouldn't be right, and I knew rather than Sean having an epiphany, he'd probably just be pissed that I was disrupting *his* tidy life.

I heard all about Sean and Nicole's elegant, yet simple wedding at a mountainside resort from one of our mutual friends. It sounded perfect, and I knew I was right not to contact him. I met Caleb two weeks later. I think I was open to finally meeting someone, because I knew that my opportunity with Sean was long gone. It was probably for the best. We both got a happy ending, just not with each other.

I start to type, *Yes, please unfriend him* and erase it. I type, *Why, Sean, why did you ever friend him in the first place?* and erase that. I drink another gulp of wine and cough a bit. Caleb took the boys to a movie this year, now that they're ten and twelve years old. It's odd that it's like a little celebration for them and they have no idea why—no idea that it's the worst day of the year for me. They just know that they get to spend time with Dad while Mom stays upstairs—a rarity. They won't be home for another hour. I can take as much time as I need to decide what to do next.

What I want to do is drink the whole damn bottle of wine and send Vin a message, tell him that even though he probably has no recollection of me whatsoever, I can never forget him. I can never forget his face or the feel of his hands pressing down on my shoulders or the pain he sent ripping through me as he thrust into me or even how he almost choked me when he shoved himself in my mouth—or the shock I felt when he dove down on me, his teeth roughly scraping delicate skin. That night was half a lifetime ago, but I'll never forget. I go to his profile and click on send a message. I type *Fuck you, you fucking piece of shit asshole*, but close it. I could never send a message, because then he would see me. He might remember me, he might not, but I never want him laying eyes on me nor on my children.

Instead of sending him a message, I click on the three dots next to send a message and down drops a box with a choice to click *Report* or *Block*. While I'm so tempted to report his profile, I can't say that I'm reporting him for something he did to me over twenty years ago—I'd need to report him for something against Facebook rules on his profile now. I click on *Block* and a box appears, warning me of all of the things Vin can't do if I block him, like see things I post on my timeline, tag me or invite me to events or groups. The best one says that he *Can't start a conversation with me*. He can't add me as a friend either. Fine by me. More than fine. I click *Confirm* and with that, Vin is blocked. I feel a rush of relief, a feeling of power. Something I couldn't do all those years ago—block him—I can do now, even if it's just virtually.

I click back on Sean's message and type, *Okay, I forgive you. Please unfriend him for me. You don't need to tell him why. He has hundreds of friends, and if you really don't keep in touch he probably won't even notice. Just do it for me. I'm sorry. You know what? I'm not sorry.. Just do it. Please.*

Not even a moment later, a message pops up, *Done. I would never want to hurt you on purpose. You know, I'll always regret the way our friendship ended back then—no matter how happy I am in my life now. The hurt in your eyes, the way you looked so fragile, like you could just snap in two, will always haunt me. I know today is the anniversary—I can't forget that date either. That night also crushed me for what it did to you, and I'm so, so very sorry that I was the cause of you seeing Vin again, even if it was just on a screen. You're a strong woman, Kate. I always thought that, and I always will. You're a survivor and that's something that Vin can never take away from you. Please remember that.*

I smile as I read Sean's message. "He's right you know," I say out loud to no one and take another sip of wine. Then, I take that rotten bit of psychic food and throw it right into the garbage—rid of it for another year.

For a moment I think about taking back down that flowered journal and burning it or at least throwing in the recycle bin. Or maybe pulling out the pages and shredding them. But then I realize that everything recorded in that journal made me who I am today. Destroying it would be destroying a part of myself. I need to own the dark parts, as well as the light. If I've learned anything, it's that tamping those dark parts down, pretending that they don't exist, is the most dangerous practice of all. So, I'll live with the knowledge that there may always be a small part of me that's broken and that's okay. Because, just like Sean said, I'm stronger than I'll ever know. I'm a survivor.

CHAPTER TWO

I BELIEVED SEAN'S words, and I thought that as soon as he unfriended Vin, I'd be done with the insidious thoughts that had started winding their way into my brain. But even as April slid into May, Vin's face kept popping up before my eyes. Actually, more than just his face—it was a whole scene. The photo from Vin's Facebook page of him leaning over the bloody shark, his menacing grin almost gleeful. That scene spun me back to the first time I starved myself.

I was eating a bowl of vegetable soup and working on an English paper when my friend, Gina's, face suddenly flashed on the TV screen with the word, "MURDERED" in bright red, ominous letters below it. I dropped my soup on the shag carpet and for weeks after, I picked little, mushy bits of alphabet pasta and carrots out of the brown fibers. Our living room smelled like vegetable soup for months no matter how much carpet cleaning powder I sprinkled on it.

Gina was murdered eight months after Vin assaulted me, and at the time I was certain that he did it. I even called in an anonymous tip to the police. Gina had told me a couple of months earlier that one day Vin asked her out after a class they had together, but because she knew what he did to me, she said no. He kept asking until she finally answered, "I don't date rapists" and walked away. When she told me he was furious and glared at her during every class after, I was already worried that he'd do something to her. But I worried he'd find some way to get her alone and assault her, too. I didn't think he'd kill her...until that night her face flashed on the news. I hadn't seen her for a couple of days, but we had plans to hit the uptown bars that weekend. The fear I felt seeing the news report, the certainty in the pit of my stomach that Vin had something to do with it...is what led me to call the police.

But despite my tip, I don't know if Vin was ever even questioned. A mentally ill homeless man, Albert Jones, admitted in a suicide note to stabbing my friend, leaving her upside down in the passenger seat of her car, and the case was closed. Gina had been shopping for Christmas gifts at the mall by herself. Her bags were still in the car, nothing was stolen. After she was killed, I imagined that perhaps she ran into Vin at the mall, and he followed her to her car. I imagined the fear she would have felt as he pushed her in the car and viciously attacked her.

Gina went to the mall late that night, maybe 9:00 p.m. or even later. It closed at 11:00 p.m., and I'd bet anything she shopped until the last minute because she told me she had a Christmas list a mile long. She had asked me to go with her, but I had too much work to do with finals that week. I was exhausted and offered her an apology and a "maybe next time," even though spending time with her was always a bright respite from work. We had met in a drawing and painting class. I took it for fun; she was an incredibly talented artist. She was working towards her BFA, and I knew that the world lost a singular vision when she was killed.

We had an instant connection and hung out most days after class, drinking tea and talking about guys, art, music, anything. I don't think I ever truly got past losing her. I barely ate for two months. But I needed to push my grief down, just like I did with my own assault...and as crocuses and daffodils tried to break through the frozen earth, I starting eating a bit more each day.

Sean helped me get through it. He insisted on "burger night" as he called it. Every Wednesday we went to the burger joint in town, and he sat with me until I got down a whole burger and a side of fries. Sometimes, I even got a big slab of chocolate frosted cake or a sweet glazed donut as big as your hand at the bakery next door. After a while, I ate more on other days of the week, too. And eventually I gave up trying to think of a way to prove that Vin killed Gina. In fact, I rarely even thought of Gina in the ensuing years. It was a sanity thing—I still missed her, but I just couldn't revisit the situation.

I would have continued along with the memory of Gina buried so deeply it would take a ton of therapy sessions to release it if I hadn't seen that photo of Vin with the shark he killed; if I hadn't seen the look of complete satisfaction on his face. Yes, I know—tons of people fish and catch sharks, and they're absolutely not homicidal maniacs. I know this. I married one of them—on our first date I noticed a photo on Caleb's bookshelf of him holding up his prizewinning catch. But he didn't have that murderous glint in his eye. Or maybe it was the lack of blood in that photo. Or the fact that the shark wasn't particularly big and could have been any run of the mill fish. Or maybe it was that it didn't look so, I don't know, freshly dead. The shark in Vin's photo had a huge sharp, silver hook in its snout and its mouth was open, eyes staring, vacant, blood pooling around. Or maybe it wasn't even dead yet. That thought filled me with even more horror. I could only imagine the fear and suffering.

And somehow, that photo brought Gina back to the surface of my thoughts. I wish that I had never looked at Vin's photos, I wish that I had never clicked on his name. But after I did, Gina started showing up in my dreams. Sometimes she begged me to help her, screaming through the closed window from the passenger seat in her car as a figure loomed up behind her. In others she just said, "Hey, you want to go to the mall?" right in my face, over and over again. Same upbeat inflection she had that night, only she asked me on the phone that night—not in person.

If she had shown up at my door, would I have been more likely to go with her? Would I have been more likely to bundle up and brave the cold because she was already there? And what if I had? Would I have ended up a victim too, murdered and left upside down in the car? Or would two of us together have deterred the vicious attack? Would the murderer have thought, *Never mind, two is too difficult. I'll look for a girl alone.* Or if the murderer *was* Vin, would he have figured he could finish the job he started with me? I'll never know for sure, but after seeing Vin with that shark, I suddenly needed to know if her murder was truly solved. A mentally ill person who was dead was a pretty easy route for the police to take—no arrests, no trial. Someone admitted it...done deal. I couldn't help but wonder if that was right or a miscarriage of justice.

I telecommute three days a week and the days I was home, I began obsessively researching the case. I needed to know if Vin should have been in jail for a very long time, instead of living his perfect tropical life. For weeks, that's all I've cared about. As everything came alive after a long New England winter and chilly spring, the trees suddenly arching over my street into a canopy of green, and the small garden planted in front of my house exploding in riotous color, all I could think about was death. It's still all I can think about. And I know it will take its toll on me soon. Even my work, my one respite, is starting to suffer.

*   *   *

My boss is a wonderful woman, but I think that her patience must be wearing thin. "Hey, Kate," she says all friendly, but I know there's a lot beneath that simple opening.

I spin around in my chair. "Good morning, Virginia. How're you doing today?"

"Fine, thanks—but I'm looking over this proposal that you emailed me earlier and some of the data regarding prospective customers for the pop-up store looks a bit off. This really isn't like you at all. Normally your assessments are spot on—every single event and launch you've worked on has run so smoothly in part because of your meticulous research beforehand."

Virginia is staring at me with such a look of deep concern that I almost want to tell her that in truth I was researching my friend's decades old murder late into the night—reading confessions and police reports on my phone so it can't be traced on my work laptop—instead of researching anything that even remotely has to do with my job. Almost—I don't *really* tell her, of course. That would be career suicide. She's kind as they come, but she doesn't suffer fools. She agreed to my telecommuting so I could be home for my kids most days with the understanding that I'd always get my work done whether I was in my cubicle or at my kitchen table. No, I need to figure out some other excuse that's completely out of my control, something that she'll sympathize with.

"So sorry, Oliver had a stomach bug last night, and I was up with him most of the night. I didn't get to finish the work I had brought home, and I have to admit, I'm a bit of a zombie myself today."

"Aww, poor guy. Tell him I hope he feels better, and I'll just send the report back to you marked up where I think there may be errors. You think you can get it back to me in a few hours?"

"Absolutely," I assure her. Quite frankly, I'm a bit terrified that my saying Oliver has a stomach bug will somehow bring the evil eye on us, crazy as that sounds.

After Virginia walks away, I even secretly bite my tongue and slap my face. I figure I could pretend to just be waking myself up if anyone happens to glance in my cubicle. It's a weird thing to do, but growing up my mom admonished, "Bite your tongue and slap your face!" at the mere mention of anything unpleasant. And I'm just far too superstitious. I guess the apple doesn't fall far from the tree.

When Virginia sends me the report, I push Gina to the back of my mind. I can't lose my job. We need the two incomes, and it's my bit of sanity. Besides my distraction with Gina, I'm a little fuzzy, because I haven't been eating much. The night before, I served everybody dinner and took a smaller plate for myself so my tiny serving wouldn't be lost on a vast white dinner size plate. Caleb hasn't noticed that I'm eating less yet, but I'm sure he will at some point. I keep telling myself it's okay because I've only lost a few pounds. Skipping breakfast today, I promised myself I'd eat at lunch. At lunch my stomach clutches, and I worry I'll get sick, so I get a corn muffin and a cup of tea from the coffee shop downstairs from my office and eat it slowly at my desk while I work on the report for Virginia.

I'm having a bit of trouble concentrating, but strange as it may sound, the fuzziness that comes with hunger is almost a relief. It blurs the edges a bit. It makes all the thoughts swirling around my head just a bit softer and less menacing. And this scares the hell out of me. I remember this feeling so clearly. I remember the comfort that slight loss of clarity gave me back when I was starving myself. It was like a drug. What else does a drug do but soften reality? Take you out of it for a bit. I notice my hands are shaking as I bring the corn muffin to my lips and know that I'm going too far. But I don't know how to stop this slide.

I hand the report in to Virginia, saying a silent prayer that I fixed everything she wanted, and explain that I have to get home for Oliver; the babysitter called, and he's feeling worse. I bite my tongue inside my mouth and slap my face as soon as I get in my car. I feel like these flimsy superstitions are all I have left. If Oliver gets sick now, I'll blame myself.

Robin, my old therapist once told me that I give my thoughts way too much power. I had confided in her that I felt like if I didn't worry about something, it would surely happen. If I didn't worry about Caleb when he went bungee jumping when we were first dating (an activity I hated), surely the cord would break and he'd slam his head against the rocks below, killed in an instant. If I didn't worry about a big presentation, I'd certainly screw up in front of a room full of people. If I didn't worry about the vicious headaches I suffered from, the doctor would tell me I have brain cancer.

Worrying felt like a talisman back then, like a smooth stone I rubbed for good luck, and only therapy taught me that whether I worried or not, whatever was going to happen would happen. My worrying didn't change the course of anything and only made my headaches worse and my life miserable. And I was so much better for so long. I still worried, of course—every mother worries. But it didn't taint everything. I tell myself that whether I bite my tongue or not, saying that Oliver has a stomach bug won't make him get one. Only germs can make him sick, not my words. And, if by some chance he does get sick, it was a kid in his class sharing germs—not my words—that caused it. I sigh. Much better.

When I get home, I pour myself a bowl of Rice Krispies. I read the nutrition information while I eat and decide that it's fortified enough that I can consider this lunch. A bowl of cereal plus a corn muffin isn't so bad. *If you're a toddler* a little voice in my head contends. "It's good enough for now," I say out loud. I know I'm losing it.

After I eat, I get on my laptop and search for cold cases in New England. Maybe Vin didn't kill Gina, but I'm certain he's done something in the decades since he got away with assaulting me. What would have stopped him from doing it again—and maybe something even worse? Nothing. There's the case of a woman who was raped and strangled after being abducted from the store she worked at in 1998. She was the same age I was that year. The case was never solved.

I search for *Vin Merdone sex offender*, but nothing comes up. How many crimes must he have gotten away with to not have any record? I don't even entertain the thought that in the years following he never attacked anyone. I'm fairly certain with the brutality he displayed with me—with the sheer sense of entitlement—that he did it again. I'd love to go confront him. Travel to Florida and track him down. Tell him that he has to pay.

I Google *Vin Merdone arrests*. The only thing that comes up is a lawsuit by a former tenant of a building he owns. She fell down the stairs and sued him, stating he didn't keep up the property and the stairs were rotted. A slumlord. That makes sense. But he was only fined. There has to be something that he paid for more dearly—something that he's done over the past two decades that landed him in jail.

I snap my laptop shut. I'm becoming obsessed, and I need to put the brakes on it. Once again, I wish that I had never laid eyes on Vin's Facebook account. It's so strange how you can push something so far down that you've almost forgotten about it—almost, you never really forget—and then boom, one little thing and it's taking over your brain like it happened yesterday. I wish I could report him now for what he did to me then, but the statute of limitations is long gone.

I manage to get down a slice of pizza for dinner, and it feels like a victory. I don't think my family has noticed anything, and for that I'm thankful. Or maybe Caleb has noticed. When we get into bed, he rolls towards me and kisses my neck. His hand is under my nightgown in a moment, sliding along my stomach. "Mmm, you feel amazing, Kate. Your stomach is so flat."

He lifts up my nightgown and plants little baby kisses from my breasts to the edge of my underwear. I'm wearing pink string bikinis and he hooks a finger under one bit of elastic and pulls them down. "Yummy," he whispers as his tongue darts into me and then circles languorously. It feels incredible, but I can't relax. I keep seeing Vin's face as it was twenty-one years ago as he dove down onto me as I tried desperately to push him away. I pull away from Caleb slightly and he grabs my hips and pulls me in closer. I writhe for a moment under his tongue, stubble pressed against me in an amazing juxtaposition of pleasure and just the slightest pain.

"That's it, Kate. Just let it go. You've been so stressed lately. You need a release." But Vin's face rises in front of me, and I just can't. I try to roll away, muttering something to Caleb about how he must be tired. One part of me wants the release, but one part is holding back. There are certain positions I've never been able to do—Caleb can't climb on top of me and be in my face. I'll give blow jobs to him freely, if I'm in control, but not if he's hovering over me and I'm on my back.

That's what Vin did after he thrust into me and hissed that I was too dry—pushed me down and crammed himself in my mouth. I thought of biting him, but I was afraid he'd kill me. I begged him to get off. I tried to push him off, but he was so much bigger—all muscle to my petite five-foot one-inch frame. Finally, he let up and told me I could finish him with my hand. It seemed like the best way out, but when he climaxed, I hated myself for doing it. It was the least invasive—he had already been in me, between my legs and in my mouth. When he roughly put his mouth on me, it was the first time anyone had done that, and until I was with

Caleb, I couldn't understand why my friends talked about oral sex like it was intoxicating. I shuddered at the thought. Using my hand seemed like my only choice. It felt detached from me and once he was done, I knew he'd let me go. But for months after, I was haunted by dreams that I chopped my own hand off and threw it away or burned it or even destroyed it in a woodchipper.

Caleb pulls me back, whispering, "I'm never too tired to take care of you. Come on, let it go."

"I can't," I wail. "I'm sorry."

"Did I do something?" Caleb's voice is laced with worry, and I immediately feel guilty. "Is it because I didn't shave? Does my stubble hurt you?" He rubs his cheek and chin. "I'll go shave right now."

"No, I love the stubble. You know that. I just… My brain isn't working right now. I'm just so tired. I don't think I'll be able to have one."

"Can you please tell me what's been going on with you, Kate? You just haven't been yourself for weeks. Normally my tongue always works its magic on you." Caleb winks at me, and I know that I'm perilously close to full-on sobs. He continues, "I haven't wanted to say anything. I just figured it was pressure from work, so I gave you space."

I don't know how to explain to him that I've been spiraling since seeing Vin's face; how knowing that he's out there and hasn't paid for his actions at all is slowly driving me crazy. "I've been having some flashbacks lately," I whisper.

"Flashbacks?"

"You know how I told you I saw that guy on Facebook, the one who attacked me in college?"

Caleb nods his head, but still looks a bit confused. "You told me you saw him, but I thought you were okay with that."

"I thought I was, too."

"But…" Caleb draws out the word and then pauses, gazing at me expectantly. I remain silent. "You're not?"

I play with a loose thread hanging off my pillowcase. We got this sheet set for our engagement party. I remember unzipping a corner of the plastic case when we registered for it and fingering the impossibly smooth fabric. I zipped it back up and admired the tiny sage green embroidered flowers before scanning it. I could just imagine all the peaceful nights we'd have slumbering on such beautiful sheets. They're so faded now from years of washing; the delicate flowers look almost mint green and the cream Egyptian cotton is now white. "We really should get new sheets," I say quietly.

"Yes, I know. We've been saying that forever, but we never do—that's not what I asked you. I didn't ask if we should get new sheets, I asked if you were okay with seeing Vin."

I don't quite know how to answer Caleb without breaking down in tears, so I don't. I just nod my head and smile at him.

"You don't seem okay. Honestly, I can't ever remember you turning down oral—not since I introduced you to the pleasures of it when we were dating." His wicked grin is almost enough to make me forget, but not quite. "You usually love it."

"I still do. Really. I'm just tired."

With that, Caleb gives up. "Okay, I won't push you. I never would."

I kiss Caleb and roll over. I mutter that I love him as I drift off into an uneasy sleep. An hour later I awake to find Caleb's side of the bed empty. The sheets are cool, so I know he didn't just wake up to go to the bathroom. I stare at the clock as it creeps past midnight.

For over half an hour I watch the minutes scroll by—I'm about to give up and get out of bed to look for Caleb when I drift off. In the morning I ask him why he got out of bed. "Hey Cal, you were gone for a while last night. Were you feeling okay? Did you have trouble sleeping and go downstairs to watch TV or something?"

Caleb focuses on slicing a banana into his Cheerios—way more concentration than a simple task requires. When he's done, he looks up and says, "Hmm? Did you ask me something?"

Just as I'm about to ask him again, Jacob comes bounding in, asking for pancakes. How about microwave pancakes?" I ask. "You have to go to school soon. No time to make real pancakes. Sorry, buddy." Oliver comes down right after Jacob, his hair sticking straight up from his forehead, eyes still sleepy, he looks so sweet and innocent; it breaks my heart just a bit. I think that was the most shocking thing about becoming a parent is how loving your kids so much can feel a tiny bit like heartbreak—you know at some point they'll leave you and you won't be able to protect them from the world outside your door. But it's your job to send them out—to school, then to college and eventually adult life. I kiss each of them on the head as I hand them their pancakes and notice that slight move to brush the kiss away. They would have giggled and kissed me right back when they were smaller. Already I'm losing them a little bit.

I pour them their juice and turn to talk to Caleb, but he's leaving for work already, and my chance to ask is gone. I make a mental note to ask him later. I don't think he's having a cyber-affair, but I haven't exactly been affectionate, and I know there are other things he might be doing. Last night he may have just gone to get a snack or something, but if I wake up tonight and he's not in bed, I'm guessing that he's been creeping down to our office to watch porn. We've been through this before—after I had the boys—and I've told him so many times that I hate porn. Having been sexually assaulted can do that to you, or at least it did that to me—and he promised he'd stop. The pain sears through me, thinking perhaps he's gone back to his habit.

I have other things on my mind, though and as soon as the boys leave for school, I go back to my research. I scroll through

all of the articles on Gina, and there it is—one that says that the
suicide note left by her supposed murderer seemed fishy. It
says that the man was mentally ill and perhaps delusional—
leading him to believe he had killed her. Her murder was all
over the news, he could have easily conjured the details in his
mind, making himself believe he had done it. I have no idea
how I can reopen what's considered a closed case—how I could
ever get anyone to believe me without a shred of evidence. I
put my head on my desk and just let the tears splash over the
wood. I don't know why I've become obsessed with this. But I
know myself, and I know that once an idea latches on, I can't
just let it go.

Apparently, I'm not the only one obsessed with a
murder—there are chat rooms and message boards full of
discussions about dead bodies—where they were found; if
they were dismembered; what clues were left; similarities to
other cases. Until I started researching Gina's murder, I had
no idea that there was such a macabre undercurrent to the
web. I stumbled upon a thread in one such chat room, Cold
Case Clues, about Gina and how her murder was similar to a
string of unsolved murders in the area, but law enforcement
(or LE as they call it on the boards) never made the
connection because that case was supposedly solved.

In the eyes of the police, Gina's murder was stand-
alone—a single act by a mentally unstable man with no
history of violence. Plus, some of those other unsolved
murders occurred after he had already killed himself. The
members on this thread were furious that "LE" didn't
pursue the similarities—didn't even give credence to the
possibility that perhaps Albert Jones admitted to a crime he
never even committed.

I click on Google and type in *Vin Merdone criminal record*.
Before I only typed in *arrests* and *sex offender*. Maybe this will
bring up more. A whole slew of sites pop up, but each one
asks me to pay, and I can't tell which are legitimate and

which will steal my credit card information, give me a virus or both. Most of them tell me there are two records I can view if I pay, which I take to mean that he was arrested three times, but it could also just be a lure to get me to pay. I decide that I need to scroll through Vin's Facebook again for more clues. I don't know exactly what kind of clues I'd find on his public profile, but I unblock him and scroll through anyway. I'm just sliding right down that rabbit hole.

One post is about a football player thug. I don't read the whole thing, but I get that he assaulted someone and got away with it. Vin's comment on the thread catches my eye, though. It says, *He's a fucking piece of garbage who should be in jail. He has no remorse.* I suck in my breath, sharp, almost a gasp. I think I might vomit. My fingers are itching to type, *You're the fucking piece of garbage. You're the one who should be in jail.* Hot tears sting my eyes, and I'm shaking. Why did I ever unblock him? Why did I ever look? He has no idea what he has done to me, if he thinks he can judge another thug; if he's acting *holier than thou.* I wish I could unsee his comment, but I can't. I know I need to bring him down, and I need help.

I quickly block Vin again and click on messages. I type, *Remember my friend Gina?* and hit send.

Sean writes back right away. *Of course. Such a tragedy. Why are you asking?*

I've been doing some research, and I really think Vin killed Gina. Do you know there are whole websites with message boards dedicated to unsolved mysteries? On one of them they talked about how Gina's murder is a lot like a string of other murders in the area in the early to mid-nineties. I drum my fingers on the desk waiting for Sean's reply. I don't know if he'll think I'm crazy. Luckily, it's just as quick as his first reply.

I know about all of those websites. I've even been contacted by some of them for forensics advice. I hate to tell you Kate, but they're often a bunch of loonies posting on those sites. These are people who have nothing better to do with their time than obsess about murders that have absolutely nothing to do with them. I mean, occasionally a family member will show up in desperation. But most of the time, it's people who just have a fascination with murder. They're amateur sleuths and usually not very good ones. Do me a favor, don't get yourself involved with them and don't take anything they say too seriously. I knew this wouldn't be easy.

I quickly type my reply, *Okay, but I went on Vin's Facebook and saw that he wrote about some football player—that the football player should be in jail. He said, 'He feels no remorse.' How can I just ignore that? I feel like I need to make him pay somehow, if he can act like he's not a piece of shit who belongs in jail. How else can I make him pay other than proving he committed these murders, including Gina?*

Sean's reply comes just a moment later, *I don't know, Kate—maybe live your life the best way you know how. Take joy in every day and don't let yourself be his victim a second time. Haven't you ever heard the phrase, 'Living well is the best revenge?' Don't do anything Kate. Forget about him as best you can, and that's how you can get back at him.*

I sigh. Sean makes perfect sense, but I just can't do that. Living well has been a great form of revenge for a long time now, but how many years did I lose before to Vin? I starved myself. I lost the possibility of me and Sean. And I could say that it wasn't meant to be because I'm with Caleb, and if I wasn't with Caleb, I wouldn't have Jacob and Oliver, and they are my heart, my life. But… I would have known what Sean and I could have been. If I wasn't so scared of letting him in, he would just be an ex-boyfriend now, not a deep well in my heart of what never was.

Sean's next message pops up. *Did I upset you? I just felt I needed to be straight with you. I'm in the business of crime and believe me no one takes those posters seriously. Just be careful.*

You didn't upset me, I answer. *I just can't let it go. I can't. I need you to help me. Can you do that?*

My phone chimes with a "VIP" email. I pick it up and glance at it. "Fuck," I whisper. It's Virginia looking for a report that was due an hour ago.

I have to run now. I need to get back to work. Just think about it, please?

Okay. You know I'd do anything for you no matter how insane. Because you know you're a little insane right now, right? But I love you anyway. He ends the message with a kiss emoji and the tight knot of fear in my stomach eases just a bit. We are always free with *I love you.* Caleb looked over my shoulder once when I was messaging Sean. "Do you guys still say, 'I love you?' in your messages?" he asked. "Didn't you break up like twenty years ago or something?"

"Sean and I never dated," I assured him. "I've told you that a bunch of times. It's like saying, 'I love you' to a girlfriend. You've heard me say 'I love you' to Heather, my old roommate, when I talk to her on the phone on our birthdays, right?" It's true—Heather and I talk to each other twice a year, but it's always like no time has passed, and we always end with, "I love you. Let's talk sooner." We never do.

"I guess. Just wondering…" Caleb trailed off. I know that he has had his suspicions about me and Sean. He doesn't quite believe me that we never slept together. Or maybe he doesn't believe me that I never wanted to sleep with him. I remember watching a television show years ago—the wife told her husband that she doesn't worry about the women he slept with in the past, only the ones he didn't sleep with. That stuck with me. I believe that URST, as they called it in my screenwriting class in college—unresolved sexual tension, the lynchpin of a successful story line—is far more dangerous than even the sexiest of exes. But I'd never act on it. I'd never cheat on Caleb. At least I tell myself that.

* * *

I spend the rest of the afternoon working on my report. It's a relief to be distracted, and I finally feel like I'm accomplishing something. I'm working on the second phase of the pop-up store launch in the center of town. It will be selling touristy items for all the naturalists who come for the mountainous scenery and families visiting the campus. We get a pretty odd mix here in town during the summer. Earthy crunchy types who are here for the music festivals on the town green and hiking on the many mountain trails sit at outdoor café tables next to wealthy suburbanites visiting the college with their kids—they love the cache of what's become a very exclusive school and extremely expensive. I would have never been able to attend if I needed the grades and the funds students need today. All through the late spring, summer and fall their Range Rovers and Mercedes SUVs clog up the charming streets, and we're going to try to cash in a bit on that.

I analyze the "big data" I've collected and check over all the market trends from the past five years in this area and in other liberal arts college towns in the region. Somehow, I manage to gather everything I've found into a coherent report with my recommendation that we go ahead and tell our client to pursue the opportunity for next spring. I hit send minutes before I need to leave to pick up Jacob and Oliver from school.

I don't have time to eat anything before I leave and, on the way, there, and I realize that all I had for breakfast was Jacob and Oliver's leftovers—two mini pancakes and half a cup of orange juice. I notice my hands are shaking a bit as I steer, and I say a little prayer that I make it to school without fainting and crashing into a tree. The school is just three minutes from my house (Lord knows I've timed it), so I get there without a problem. But when I get out of the car to meet them at the walker door, my knees buckle a bit, and everything gets speckly. *I just stood up too fast*, I think. But I have to grab at the car door as I'm about to go down. It's too late. Crumbling to the asphalt, I yell out, "Someone get my boys."

When I open my eyes, the nurse is standing over me. I sit up a bit too quickly and feel like I'm going back down. I shake it off and try to stand. "Mrs. Berg, are you okay?" she asks kindly. "Please, sit back down. I don't want you fainting again."

"I'm fine—I just didn't eat enough today." *Or yesterday or the day before that*, I want to add, but I stay quiet.

"Well, I called an ambulance. They should be here any minute."

"I don't need an ambulance, just a Snickers." The nurse doesn't even crack a smile. "Seriously, I just have to take my boys home. Where are they? Someone got them at the door, right? How long was I out for?" I panic for a moment thinking that in all the commotion, they wandered off and got abducted. A bit ridiculous I know—they're ten and twelve—but still…

"Only a minute or two. I was right by the front door and someone grabbed me to come out here. And yes, a teacher brought them inside."

"Thank God."

"No need to worry." I'm so grateful that she doesn't make me feel like a crazy parent worrying about my sixth and fourth graders. She's indulging me like they're first graders and need constant supervision.

"Thank you. I really appreciate your taking care of them."

"No need to thank me. But you're welcome. They're in the auditorium with the childcare kids. Another teacher went inside to call your husband. I'm sure he can take them home if you need to go to the hospital. He works close by, right? I know he's picked your boys up before when they've been sick."

"Yes, he works in town, but I don't need to go to the hospital—really. I just need to eat something." We were both thrilled when Caleb landed a job as a financial advisor at an investment firm right in town. Before, he was commuting three hours a day—roundtrip—to Boston. He moved here for me when we got engaged but kept his job. In reality, the move wasn't for me. He moved here because we couldn't afford any houses close to his job in Boston, so we decided he'd commute while looking for a job closer to home. He ended up making the daily trip for over a decade. I'm definitely grateful he's close by today. "I really don't need an ambulance; I'm sure my husband will be here any minute."

As I'm saying that, the ambulance arrives, lights blazing. The paramedics lift me easily onto a gurney as I protest. "Ma'am, please just stay calm and quiet. We're here to help you," the twenty-something paramedic says soothingly.

"My kids are in the auditorium. I can't just leave them here. I promise—I'm fine," I insist.

"Why don't you let us determine that," the paramedic insists, and he quickly pushes my sleeve up and takes my blood pressure.

"Your pressure is ninety over fifty and your pulse is 120. You're probably dehydrated. You likely have low blood sugar, too." He cleans my finger with an alcohol pad and then sticks it so quickly I don't even notice.

"I'm okay, really," I assure him as he places a drop of blood on a test strip and sticks it in a blood sugar meter.

"Your blood sugar is forty-five. Take these right now." He hands me two flat, pale yellow tablets. I chew one and then the other as he looks on in concern. "Are you hypoglycemic? Or diabetic—have you taken insulin today?"

"I may be hypoglycemic," I answer. "I don't know. I did have some blood sugar issues when I was pregnant, I think. I remember it dropped low when I did the gestational diabetes test—you know when you drink that super sugary stuff. The doctor just told me to have snacks with me all the time—stuff with protein." The paramedic nods, and I add, "To tell you the truth, I haven't even thought about it since then."

"Do you faint a lot?"

"No. I just haven't had anything to eat today—or at least not much. I was busy working and just never had a chance."

"Ma'am, you need to eat, especially if you're driving. You could've gotten into an accident. You need to drink more water, too. Here, take this." He hands me an electric blue sports drink. "It's from my personal stash," he winks at me. He's endearingly handsome, and I almost wish he would stop calling me 'ma'am.' It makes me feel old.

I sip it slowly. It tastes like crap—what I would imagine plastic would taste like if you could drink it—but, with each sip the dizziness is ebbing away.

"Look," I begin and check his nametag before continuing. "Mike... I can't go to the hospital if you're thinking that. My kids are in the school. I need to get them and take them home."

"I can't let you drive until your pressure is back to normal and your blood sugar is up. The glucose tablets should be working already, and if you keep drinking, your blood pressure should be closer to normal soon, too. But you need to just sit here and not move. Your blood sugar should be close to normal within about fifteen minutes."

A look of frustration must cross my face because he says more softly, "Your kids will be fine. I'm sure they're being looked after. Is someone coming here to meet you?"

"The nurse said a teacher called my husband, but he's not here yet. Not sure when he will be."

At that moment, Caleb pulls into the parking lot. "There he is." I lift my chin towards Caleb's car. "Perfect timing. So, can I go home now?"

"Not so fast. Let me check your blood pressure and sugar. And remember, you have to eat some protein as soon as you get home," he instructs me, concern lacing his voice. "That glucose tablet will make you crash pretty soon if you don't eat some. And if you're hypoglycemic, always keep nuts or a protein bar or even string cheese in your purse. The glucose tablets are for an emergency like this, so you should have a roll of those too, but don't eat them like a snack. You need real food."

"You know a lot about this," I say.

"Well, I'm an EMT. And my girlfriend is hypoglycemic. Damn near crashed the car more than once when she has had an episode." Mike sighs and shakes his head in frustration. "She's a skinny little thing like you. I tell her to always keep snacks on hand. She needs to put some meat on her bones, but she's always watching what she eats." Mike shakes his head again as he sticks my finger, draws a drop of blood and checks it. He seems satisfied with the numbers. Ninety-eight over sixty for my blood pressure and sixty-six for my blood sugar—not perfect, but not terrible.

I wonder if his girlfriend is like I was when I was young, starving herself. *Or like I am right now.* It's an electric bolt that hits me. I'm slipping back—dangerously so. I know if I continue on this path, I'll wreck not only myself, but my family as well. Fainting when I have to pick my kids up *should* be a big wake-up call. I only hope it is. I tell myself that my kids are more important than anything, and if I don't get a grip, they'll lose their mother. Maybe not entirely—maybe it won't kill me, *maybe*. But they'll certainly lose me emotionally. Not eating makes me irrational, fuzzy and unable to cope with even the smallest difficulties. I can't go there again. I just wish I had the confidence in myself to know that I won't.

CHAPTER THREE

CALEB INSISTS ON driving me home, even though Mike says I'm fine to drive. We leave my car at the school to pick up later. "I'm concerned about you," he says as soon as I slide in and buckle up. "What if that had happened when you were alone with the kids? What if you hit your head?"

"Jacob and Oliver can call 911 if they had to. They're not babies."

"That's not the issue, Kate. If you fainted while you were home alone, and there wasn't anyone there—like the nurse—you may not have been okay. How about this, what if you were driving with the kids in the car when you fainted? You could have crashed and killed all of you."

"I only fainted because I stood up too quickly when I got out of the car."

"You have an excuse for everything, don't you? Okay—what's your excuse for this one… Why didn't you eat today? Was it because of what we talked about last night? The guy you saw on Facebook?"

"I want a Facebook," Jacob says from the back seat.

"Not yet," I answer, glad for the distraction.

"Why not? All of my friends have one. Why can't I?"

"I don't know. You just can't, okay? The minimum age is supposed to be thirteen. You're not thirteen yet."

"That's crazy. All of my friends have one. You're crazy."

"What did you just call me, Jacob?"

"I said you're crazy."

"You're twelve, not seventeen—you're not supposed to be talking like that yet."

"If the shoe fits…" Caleb says under his breath.

I whip my head around to face him. "Caleb!"

"I didn't say anything, Kate," Caleb insists, staring straight ahead.

Am I going crazy? Did I imagine what he said? I'm beginning to think my grasp on reality is slipping, then I see the slight smirk play across Caleb's lips, and I know that I didn't imagine it. Bastard.

"Sure, Jacob. You can make a Facebook account." I have bigger battles to fight. "But you need to give me the password and have me as a friend. I need access to everything you're doing."

"Thanks, Mom! I'm sorry I said you're crazy."

That was easy. I guess he's still at the age where he doesn't hate me all the time yet. I was worried there for a moment. Caleb is another story. I don't know why he would say something so nasty. It's not my fault that I haven't been eating. It's not my fault that seeing Vin has thrown me for a loop. "Caleb, we need to talk later."

He just stares ahead.

After I get the kids to bed, I sit down on the couch next to Caleb and turn off the baseball game. He slides me a look. "The Sox will still be on in a few minutes, Cal. I want to talk to you for just a minute."

"What, Kate? Do you want to actually talk about what happened today? Do you want to talk about how you haven't been yourself in a while? Will you finally tell me what's going on with you?"

"I'll tell you what's not going on—I'm not crazy, and I'm pissed that you would suggest otherwise, especially in front of our children. How dare you?"

"I was just being funny—I didn't think you'd even hear."

"Well, I did hear it, and I wasn't too happy about it. Why would you say, 'If the shoe fits?' You make me not want to tell you anything."

"Look—I'm sorry. I don't know what's going on with you. All I know is that I had to leave right before an important meeting with a client who, by the way, was planning on investing a big chunk of change, because you couldn't take five minutes to eat something."

"Sorry to inconvenience you," I snap.

"Okay, forget I said that," Caleb says softly and shakes his head ruefully. "I'm just really worried about you, Kate."

"You'd never know it. Mocking me isn't the way to show that you're worried. A little compassion would be nice."

"How about a little honesty from you? You act like everything is fine. I asked you if you were okay after seeing that guy, and you said you were. So, what's going on with you, Kate? Are you okay or not?"

"I'm not. Happy? I'm not okay."

"Why didn't you just say that in the first place?"

"Because you like things easy, and I'm not easy right now. I haven't been eating, and I'm terrified I'm going to slip back into the problems I had before I met you." I bite my lip and look away. I don't want to cry in front of Caleb. The only person I ever felt like I could cry in front of was Sean. I don't know why I feel so naked when I cry. I've been like that for as long as I can remember, but it's gotten worse.

"I don't only like things easy—I'm willing to listen to your problems. I think you should know that by now."

"How would I know that, Caleb? When have I ever complained to you about anything?"

"When you were pregnant you complained about your back. And that you were tired. You complain about the kids not behaving—right when I walk in the door sometimes."

"I'm not talking about tiny everyday grievances—I'm talking about big life stuff. I try to take things in stride—don't you think? I try to be easy."

"You are easy, but you don't have to be. What were you doing today that you didn't eat?"

I'm so nervous about telling Caleb, which I know is just wrong, because I told Sean without even thinking twice. I take a deep breath before diving in. "Okay—please promise you won't think I'm crazy."

"I promise." Caleb had taken off his glasses to clean them, but he puts them down with the cloth and is staring right into my eyes. I gaze back into his—they are still my favorite part of him. I could drown in them. That almost sea glass green still draws me in just like the first time we met at Percolating Paradise. They're even more striking now that the thick mahogany waves he sported when I first laid eyes on him have been replaced by a close-cropped cut with a lot more salt than pepper. He puts his hand on my knee, and I have to think that he's telling the truth. I have to think that he won't judge me or I *will* go crazy.

"I told you that I've been having some flashbacks, right?" Caleb nods. "Well, they're not only about Vin, Cal. I've also been thinking about my friend from college who was murdered, Gina. She was killed about eight months after Vin attacked me, and I always thought that maybe he killed her."

"I remember that murder case. It was all over the news because she was from the Boston area. I didn't realize you were friends with her."

"I was," I say softly.

"I'm sorry. I thought they caught the guy, though. Or didn't someone confess to the crime in his suicide note? I thought the case was closed."

"It is closed, but a lot of people think he may have been delusional. He was mentally unstable, and he could have just convinced himself that he killed her. There was no real evidence pointing to him. What if he didn't kill her and the real murderer went free?"

"Who are these people who believe that he didn't kill her? And why is this coming up all of the sudden? You never talked about her before. That happened two decades ago." Caleb's voice isn't accusatory, just confused.

"It was a photo I saw on Vin's Facebook. He was holding up a shark he had killed. There was blood pooled under the shark, and Vin had this cruel glint in his eye, a murderous satisfaction."

"So, you think that because he 'murdered' a shark, he murdered your friend? It's called fishing, Kate. People do it all the time. I've caught sharks, and I've never murdered anyone. And again…these people you're referring to, who are they?"

"I knew you'd make me feel like an idiot. I wish I never said anything. The people are on unsolved crime message boards. There are a lot of them. I Googled Gina when she popped into my head, and all these boards came up saying that they think the case should be reopened, that they don't think the guy who confessed to it, Albert Jones, really did it."

"Kate, those boards are probably filled with conspiracy nuts. You know that don't you? Don't let yourself get pulled into it. I'm sure you have better things to be doing while the kids are at school. Don't you have work to do?" The condescension dripping from his words wounds me deeply. Caleb is so smart—high-minded ideas, perfect grammar—he has no patience for things he deems useless. He takes off his glasses and rubs the bridge of his nose—his exasperated gesture.

"Never mind, Caleb. You asked me what I was doing, and I told you. I was also working, of course. I finished the report for the pop-up store in town. The one I've been working on for a while. It'll probably be open in the late spring and summer next year—seems like it would be a great project."

"Now, that's a good thing to focus on—work. I think a pop-up store in town would be great. Inject a bit of energy in the town when it's a little quieter in the summer—all hippies and rich kids visiting. Good job."

"Thanks. Good night. I'm exhausted and going to bed."

"Night. Love you. Did you eat anything tonight? Why don't you have a snack before you go to bed?" Caleb's concern just irritates me since five minutes before he was making me feel stupid—whether he meant to or not.

"I ate dinner. I'm not really hungry right now." I did eat more for dinner than I have been. Today was a bit of a wake-up call. I need to get a handle on things before they spiral out of control.

"Eat some ice cream, Kate." Caleb is reaching for the remote to turn the television back on, but he pauses and turns back to me. "Is this because I told you your stomach felt flat last night and that you looked good? Are you trying to lose weight and then when I said that..." he trails off.

"No, not at all," I assure him before he can finish. "I'm not worried about being skinny. I don't care about my weight that much." I can't tell if Caleb is relieved by that or a tiny bit disappointed. Then he sighs.

"Oh good. I don't want you to feel like you have to lose weight. I wouldn't want you to become anorexic or anything."

"I'm not anorexic. I promise I'll eat more."

"I have an idea," Caleb says with a suggestive raise of his eyebrow. "How about we work up an appetite?"

"Um," I glance around the room as I try to formulate an excuse. I just am not in the mood to let Caleb in right now— emotionally or physically. Maybe if he had been a bit more understanding I would feel more amorous.

I can't tell Caleb that, though. "You know, I would love to, but I'm getting a migraine." I rub my left temple for effect. I've become a cliché.

"No problem," Caleb says with a sigh. "I totally understand. Your migraines are killers. Sorry you're getting one. Go get some rest."

"Do you want to come to bed with me? We could at least cuddle a bit."

"I'll come to bed soon. I'm going to watch the end of the Sox game, and I might try to catch up on work a bit." Of course, he's staying up—probably for the same reason he got out of bed the night before.

I want to say, "When you say work, do you mean porn?" But I don't. I just don't have the energy to get into it right now. And if I'm pretending to have a migraine, I don't know if I even have the right to say anything, as much as it bothers me.

"Okay. Good night. Love you." I lean over the couch and kiss Caleb on the cheek. I know it's not even close to being enough, and I feel so guilty. I'm sure our lack of intimacy is why he's choosing the Sox and "work" over me. He was more than ready to come to bed if sex was on the table. I never thought we'd be like this. When we first got married, we couldn't keep our hands off of each other. Therapy helped me open up sexually, and I was making up for lost time, I think. We would even be late to parties because we had to stop to have sex before walking out the door. We'd do it on a dining room chair, in the office, in Caleb's desk chair. Any surface was good enough—we rarely made it to our bed, we hungered for each other so.

Of course, our sex life slowed down when we had kids, but it was still one of the best parts of us. No matter what—a little fight, a sick kid, a million household chores—we always made time to come together. But I realize, as a slight veil of despair falls over me, that this is probably the longest we've ever gone without sex. It's been weeks. And I don't know how to change it. It's like going to the dentist; the longer you put it off the harder it is to finally just do it. I tell myself tomorrow is another day. I'll eat more. I'll call my old therapist and make an appointment, if she's still even practicing—if not, I'll find someone new. I won't let this beat me. I won't go back down that road. Although, I know deep down that my journey back to the darkest part of me has already started.

As I'm trying to fall asleep, Vin's Facebook comment keeps looping through my brain. I wish there was a way that I could tell him what a hypocrite he is – what "a piece of garbage" he is, just like the football player he's yapping about. And then it hits me – I'll make a Facebook alias. He never has to see me at all. I can just create a new email account and create a Facebook account under that. It only takes me a moment to think of a name – Jane Doe.

I am every woman who has been violated, and I'll make my voice heard. Some people might think it's cowardly of me to hide behind a fake screen name, one that's tantamount to being anonymous. But I can't let Vin see the real me— ever. Who knows, maybe other women will come out of the woodwork if I just open the door. Of course, I'd come forward publicly if I ever needed to—if he ends up accused of any other crimes. The statute of limitations has expired long ago for me, but maybe not for others, and I'd be more than happy to tell my story to help them.

CHAPTER FOUR

THE NEXT MORNING, I feel lighter than I have in ages. I have work to do, but first I create Jane Doe. For a moment I worry that I won't be able to do it—that it too clearly smacks of anonymity, but when I search for Jane Doe on Facebook, there already is one—albeit with no posts and no profile photo. I try to decide if I should use a profile photo of something encapsulating violence, but I decide it's better to just let it be.

Once it's set up, I search for Vin and scroll down to the comment thread on his post about the football player he called a "piece of garbage who should be in jail." Every time I look at his Facebook, my insides are in a vice grip, and I know I'm in danger of vomiting all over my laptop. But I need to do this—I need to say my piece, even if I am a complete coward.

You're the fucking piece of garbage who should be in jail, I type quickly. *You're the rapist. I know what you did in college.* I hit enter before I can change my mind. And then I wait. I know it will draw him in. I imagine Vin sweating, wondering who Jane Doe is and how does she know his secret. There is nothing on my account to betray me. No friends. No other posts. I panic that he could find my IP address and identify me from it, but that seems so complex to me, and I just want immediate gratification, so I easily push it out of my mind.

I get to work on my next project—a summer music series on the Green. Everything I work on is at least a year out or more. Sometimes it gives me something to look forward to, sometimes it just makes it seem like the days until I reach the events I've planned so hard for are interminable. I try to remember that the projects I worked on last year for this summer will come to fruition soon: an "Art in the Park" festival; a kids' concert series; a collaboration between summer students in hospitality and tourism and local hotels and restaurants—"A Taste of Rolling Green." That event in June should be an amazing kick-off to the tourist season. It was my baby last year—I worked long hours to get the logistics down and to figure out the feasibility of turning the town commons into one big outdoor food hall. Now it's just weeks away. For a moment I contemplate where the past month has gone—it's already May. Soon school will be done, and the kids will be home for the summer.

I realize that the last month I've just been going through the motions of my life—not truly engaged. I try to remember all of the spring activities that must have come and gone— did I miss the spring concert and the school picnic? I've never missed either. I frantically check my phone calendar and see that they are both next week. I tell myself I haven't missed anything big yet. My obsession with Vin and my fuzziness haven't derailed me yet. *There's still time*, a tiny voice in my head whispers, and I literally swat it away.

I check my new Facebook account and there is a notification—it can only be one thing. *Vin Merdone also commented on his status.* My heart threatens to pound out of my chest as I click on it. *Who the fuck is this? I'm reporting you. You are a fucking liar. You better hope I don't find out who you are...* My hand flies over my mouth, and I barely make it to the bathroom as I vomit. After, I just sit on the floor next to the toilet for what seems an eternity.

What was I thinking? Suddenly, I'm sure that Vin can find me through my comment. I accomplished what I wanted—let him know that I'm onto him, so I quickly go back on my laptop and delete Jane Doe. If she's gone, Vin can't find me.

I'm so ashamed that I'm not brave enough to confront Vin...at least not yet. I go on my real Facebook and click on Vin's profile. I need to unblock him one more time to see if he deleted my comment. It's still there, but I suppose that if he deleted it, his reply would make no sense. One of his friends, Mike Grady, has replied, *You better be careful. The past can't stay in the past forever, Bro. We all know you were a fucked up drunk.* He added a laughing emoji.

What the fuck are you talking about, Mike? I never did shit, Vin replied just a moment later. I click on Mike's profile and sure enough, he went to college with us. Now I remember him vaguely—he was one of the *case-in-a-day guys* who just drank school away. Now he's a lawyer. I guess he outgrew his drinking habits enough to graduate law school. I do remember he was a happy drunk. Always laughing and ribbing people. Apparently, he knew what happened to me and finds it funny now. What an asshole. Or maybe, he knows about someone else.

Dude, you're just lucky you don't have a wife to beat the crap out of you or take you for everything if your past comes back to haunt you. You sure as hell have a lot to lose, Mr. Millionaire. No worries though, the statute of limitations has long passed. And if anything comes up now that can get you in trouble, you have my number. I need a nicer car—I'll get you off for sure. Not like they did, though. Another laughing emoji. I quickly take a screenshot. This all might come in handy. He wrote, "they." I wasn't the only one. It's a good thing I took the screenshot, because in another split second the entire post is gone. When I hit refresh, it just says that the link may be broken, or I may not have permission to view it. Vin either made it *friends only*, or if he was smart, deleted it completely.

It doesn't matter—I know now for sure that I'm not crazy, and I know that there were others just like me. I text Sean right away to tell him my news.

He replies immediately, *I'll dig around a bit and let you know if I find any other accusations or anonymous reports. Why don't you let me do the research and you try to get back to your life?*

I answer, *Okay, I'll try.* But I don't know if I will. I still don't know if Vin killed Gina, but I'm putting that on the back burner for now. My best bet to bring him down is to find the other women he assaulted—I know that they're out there, thanks to Mike Grady. I don't know exactly how finding the other women will bring him down—Mike Grady is right, the statute of limitations has passed, and Vin doesn't have a family to worry about. But, according to Mike, he's a millionaire, and he *does* have something to lose. I knew his lifestyle looked lavish, but I had no idea that he's a millionaire. So, I do go down the rabbit hole of Googling how he made his money and wallowing in anger, until I glance at the time and gasp, snapping my laptop shut.

Somehow, it's crept past noon, and I haven't gotten any work done. I'm running out of excuses for Virginia. I can't keep saying my kids have a stomach bug, so I work non-stop until the boys come home. As soon as they walk in, I say brightly, "Who wants some frozen yogurt?"

A resounding yes from both boys sends us back out the door. Fear wraps its fingers around me as soon as we enter the cool, turquoise and pink shop. I had planned on getting yogurt and at least one or two toppings, but I don't think I can. My stomach lurches just thinking about it sliding down my throat. I know it will make me sick, even though they have my favorite—toasted marshmallow. They don't always have that—the flavors revolve—but whenever they do, I usually get it. But of course, that was...before.

"Mom, Mom, they have toasted marshmallow!" Oliver shares excitedly, pulling me over to the machine.

"Grab a cup, buddy." I say as cheerfully as I can manage.

I sit down while the boys fill their cups and dump on topping after topping. Each yogurt will probably cost $8 or even $10, but I don't care. "Mom, aren't you going to have any?" Oliver asks sweetly.

"I would love to Honey-Bun, but my stomach is a little off today."

Jacob chimes in, "Big deal. It's your favorite. So, you take a dump after. I just unloaded a huge one before we left."

Twelve-year-old boy logic is actually flawless in this situation. Jacob is right. I might just need to "take a dump," as he put it. Really…what *is* the big deal? I want to set a good example for my boys and not be eaten alive by anxiety over this, so I say, "You're right, Jacob, I'll get some."

I fill a cup halfway with toasted marshmallow frozen yogurt and top it off with M&M's and Reese's Peanut Butter Cups just for good measure. It's delicious, but it feels like lead going down my throat. "Mmm! This is sooo yummy!" I say too cheerfully. "Do you guys like yours?"

"Yeah. Do you like *yours*?" Jacob eyes me warily. "Because it seems like you don't. It seems like you don't like much anymore."

It is a punch in the gut to realize that Jacob has noticed that I haven't been eating. I manage to get down a few more bites, but even knowing that my kids are watching me, even knowing that I need to be a pillar of strength in front of them, I can't get down *more* than a few bites. And it kills me.

You would think that moment would be a turning point. You would think that wanting to get better for my kids would cut through the anxiety and propel me to healthy eating, but it didn't. The weeks rolled by with more unfinished meals, more scattered days. Even though Sean eventually convinced me to stop spending hours researching

Vin—he promised he would let me know if he found anything—Vin still distracted me, lurking in the corners of my mind, taunting me with his perfect life on Facebook. Eventually, I blocked him again…but the damage was done.

I fell behind in work, and Virginia suggested that I take a leave of absence to deal with whatever it was that was ripping me apart. I haven't worked in three weeks. She promised me she'd just hire a temp so I could have my job back when I returned from the abyss. I believe her. But I just don't know if I can get to the other side.

This is what's going through my head when Caleb suddenly asks, "Why don't we visit your parents this weekend?" It's innocuous enough, but it seems to me like something is bubbling up beneath the surface. We're sitting on the couch—the boys have all finally gone to bed, and the house is quiet. I'm flipping through a magazine, barely noticing the pages of glossy perfection. Caleb is watching the Red Sox. Sex has faded away for us. Caleb doesn't even bother asking anymore, which is both a relief and impossibly sad.

I gaze at him suspiciously—he has never once suggested we visit my parents. He dislikes going to Long Island. He thinks everyone has an attitude and the traffic sucks. I miss home so much sometimes it's visceral, so I'm afraid if I go, I won't want to leave. I love my little college town, my adopted home, but the expanse of ocean on one side and the stretch of Sound with Connecticut in the distance on the other calls to me at times. I also miss the Chinese food and bagels the size of your head. Oh, and the pizza…I can wax poetic about the puffy, golden crust enrobed in ruby sauce and topped with rich, silken mozzarella that stretches tantalizingly between crust and lips with every bite. Maybe if I still lived at home I would weigh more—but I doubt it. I'd find some excuse not to eat probably, as tempting as everything is… "Okay. Sounds good," I answer. "Do you want to stay with my parents or book a hotel room?"

"We'll stay with your folks. Maybe we can go away overnight to the Hamptons—just get away."

"That sounds fantastic," I practically purr as I lean over and kiss Caleb's neck, working my way up to his ear. I give it a little nibble. If he is making the effort to plan a getaway, I can certainly try to be a little sexy. But he seems uncomfortable, so I back away, a bit wounded.

Two days later we're on our way to Long Island, sitting in endless traffic on the Hutchinson Parkway when Oliver says out of the blue, "I'll miss you when you're away, Mommy."

"I'm not going anywhere, honey. But thank you. Daddy and I were going to go away for a night, but we never planned it. Plus, I'll always be right by your side—or at least until you're bigger and don't want me there, which is how your brother is getting. I shoot a glance at Jacob. He looks stricken.

"I'll miss you too, Mom."

I glance at Caleb, bewilderment creeping into dread as I notice his hands gripping the steering wheel tighter, knuckles blanching. "What are they talking about, Caleb?" the panic is rising in my voice. And then...then I remember that I saw Caleb load an extra bag into the trunk, a larger suitcase. I didn't think too much about it—I thought maybe he just packed a little more than usual, or maybe he had a surprise for me for our trip. A gift—maybe a stack of books or a new sweater or something. I don't know why I thought it was something positive. I don't know why I thought we would hit the reset button this weekend and emerge stronger than before. Whom was I kidding? Myself, apparently.

Oliver is the first one to spill, "Daddy said you're going to go away for a little bit to get better. He said they'll teach you how to eat more and maybe to forget about the things that have been making you sad. I hope it helps you. I don't want you to be sad anymore."

"Dad says we can't visit you too much, but that you'll be home soon," Jacob offers. "We're going to stay with

Grandma and Grandpa while he takes you to the place that'll help you get better."

"Dad also said not to say anything to Mom, so he could tell her himself, but apparently that didn't sink in, did it?" Caleb says bitingly.

There is an edge of anger in Jacob's answer that I haven't heard in his voice before, not the whiny anger of young children, but a more righteous anger—the anger of those who have been misled, betrayed. "You said you were going to tell Mom so she wasn't surprised that you're just leaving her somewhere. You promised that it wouldn't be a surprise. You know Mom hates surprises. I thought it would be fine to say something now. Don't blame me." I hear the teenager in Jacob's voice. It's deeper and cracks on a word or two. I wonder when that happened and how I missed it. How long have I been out of it? Perhaps I do need help, and Lord knows I wouldn't willingly go. Maybe Caleb is right in doing this.

I turn around from the front seat and address the boys directly, their solemn faces make me want to weep, but I hold it together somehow—at least for a moment. They look so different...mini-me Oliver with his ginger curls and hazel "tiger eyes" and Jacob with his wavy chestnut mop and sea glass green eyes just like Caleb's. The sun is streaming in the windows of the minivan, turning Oliver's hair an almost golden apricot and gracing Jacob's with threads of copper. I just stare at them for a moment, taking them in before everything changes—before I can't see their beautiful faces for I don't know how long...

I take a deep breath and make my voice as bright and chipper as possible, "Guys, thank you so much for saying you'll miss me and for worrying about me. I love you both so much—I want you to know that. And I would never want to leave you. But maybe Dad is right. Maybe I do need some help in learning to eat better." The tears are threatening to spill right over my lashes, leaving a trail down my cheeks, so I quickly turn back and face ahead.

Caleb reaches across the console and takes my hand in his. He squeezes it and whispers, "This is the first step to getting you back. You've been physically present, but not really here. We miss you."

It's funny how a tiny moment can change one's perspective. I've been so wrapped up in myself that I didn't even notice how my family might be suffering. I didn't think about why Caleb escaped to his office at night—only that he did. Suddenly realizing that Jacob's voice has been changing, and I didn't even notice, was like a knife in my chest, a wake-up call that I need to change something. I need to get better. My family has been missing me? I had no idea. And now, because of me, they'll miss me even more. And I'll miss so much. I'll miss baseball games and family walks and maybe even sixth grade graduation. "How long will I be there?" my voice is barely a whisper, as I choke back tears.

"That's up to you," Caleb replies quietly, but with hope in his voice. "If you do the work that's needed, it could be just a few weeks. If not, it could be a few months."

"No, no, no...I'm not going away for months. I thought it would be a week or two. Isn't there a program in Massachusetts I could go to—one where you can visit me? Isn't there a day program I could try first? You know, I'm an adult, I can refuse to go to a residential program." I suddenly regret that I signed the papers at my last physical stating that the doctor could talk to Caleb. I just always write his name in the blank on the privacy form and don't give it a second thought.

"That's true. You could have refused. You could still refuse. But I hope you'll realize that I did this because I love you. We love you. And it will help you come back to us. Even though you're here, you're not really *here*."

I think about this for a moment. I could refuse, but if I keep getting worse, what will that do to my kids? Will I get to the point that I'll end up in the hospital, the decision out of my hands? "There's nothing closer?"

"Not that takes our insurance—since it's my plan, I was able to find out coverage, and this was the best option." Caleb pauses, then adds brightly, "Plus, this one is on the beach. You know how much you love the beach. You always say it's what you miss the most about Long Island. They take beach walks every day and hold sessions by the ocean. Meditation and yoga. I think you'll love it."

"I won't love anything that's away from my family. Maybe if you all were with me, I'd love it."

"Your parents and sisters said they'll visit you. Your friends who are still here will visit. I talked to Heather, she'll come. And we'll come out at least one weekend. But I think it's better if you do this on your own. Maybe I stress you out…" his voice trails off.

"So, all these people knew about this, but I didn't?" I feel exposed, naked, that everyone knows what I've been going through. To know that they've been talking about me, discussing my issues and probably helping Caleb decide how best to get me into treatment just fills me with despair. I know I should appreciate that they care enough to do this and to keep it a secret, but the secrecy feels like a betrayal.

"I can't believe you discussed this with everyone but me."

"Really? No thank you for caring about you enough to do this? No wondering how much work it was to get you into a top-notch program and line up insurance coverage because otherwise we would have had to sell our house? No thought at all about how you not eating has been affecting your children? That perhaps fainting at pick-up should have been a wake-up call? No consideration of any of that—just anger at me for doing something to get you better?"

I'm silent, staring at the window, hoping my children don't see me cry…and hoping they'll forgive me someday.

"That's what I thought," Caleb says quietly. "That just proves how much you need this."

I turn around and face my boys, ignoring Caleb to address them directly. "I'm so sorry. I hope someday you'll forgive me." And then for perhaps the first time ever, I let them see me cry.

CHAPTER FIVE

"IF YOU'RE GOING to ask the universe for forgiveness and a reset, I guess sunrise on the ocean is the right time and place to do it." I shrug and turn to my *Morning Mantra* partner, Rose, "Right?"

"Right," she agrees.

Every activity here at Serenity Cove has a name, and it's usually some catchy alliteration. It's never just a walk on the beach or yoga in the solarium or lunch on the patio or dinner in the sumptuous dining room. It's *Morning Mantra, Serenity Stretching, Mindfulness Meals* or *Dining Without Distractions*. We have our phones for two half hour breaks a day, and that is it. The outside world retreats, and we are ensconced in a fake universe of constantly sunny "peer counselors" who tell us over and over again that they've been in our shoes and have come out stronger. A universe where every meal is prepared by a culinary institute-trained chef and eaten with heavy sterling silver forks, and the crystal goblets we lift to our lips filled with the ever-present calorically dense, disgusting tasting nutrition supplement seem heavier than some of the clients.

Everywhere I look, I see jutting collarbones, sunken cheekbones, arms like the delicate bones of devoured chicken wings that look like they could snap with the lightest touch. I didn't think I looked like *that* until I was forced in a therapy session to look at myself...really look. It was horrifying. It was the first step to getting better. I ate a whole chicken breast over spinach and angel hair with garlic olive oil at dinner that night. Rose gazed at me as I ate the last bite. I could see the envy invading her features. Her food sat mostly untouched. You could see looking at her what a beauty she had been before she stripped it all away. Crystal blue eyes and strawberry blonde curls that cascade down past the middle of her back when she didn't wrap them up in a tight bun. A smattering of freckles across her nose. But her skin hangs from her bones, like a silk dress on a hanger. She was here my first day, and I fear for her that she'll be here long after I leave.

Today is day thirteen. Lucky thirteen. I'm hoping that today is the day they tell me I can go home, but I know my hopes will be dashed again. Starting around the fifth day, the morning after I ate the whole chicken breast for the first time, I started hoping they'd release me. I would just sign myself out, after all, I'm an adult, but I have no way of getting home, no money, no phone unless I can figure out where they locked it up. Nothing. And the days have stretched and tumbled into one another until I'm on the cusp of two weeks away from everything I love.

The day Caleb dropped me off I cried and cried. I felt like a small child, abandoned. I was so embarrassed that I hid in my room pretending to unpack for over an hour. I didn't want anyone to see my puffy eyes and red nose. I tried to stay in the bathroom, but that isn't allowed. Someone stands at the door, listening to you to make sure that you're actually using the toilet and not vomiting. I tried to explain that I'm afraid of vomiting and would never make myself do it, but they didn't care. I tried to explain that I don't want to be skinny, I just don't want to feel sick, but, again, they didn't care. Anything I said was viewed suspiciously. So, I learned to stay quiet. I talk to Rose, because we share a room—and because she seems even more shattered than I am.

"How long have you been here?" I asked the first night.

"Too long."

"Where are you from?"

"Nowhere."

I stared at the ceiling trying to think of what to say next.

"I don't eat because I want to disappear," she whispered into the darkness. But I heard, and I understood.

"I think everyone wants to disappear at some point. At least everyone here does." There are only six of us, six of us in a huge mansion in the Hamptons...all women in our twenties, thirties and forties. I had heard that a woman in her seventies was released the day before I arrived. The thought of still battling this in thirty years filled me with despair and resolve to beat it.

Every night I called my boys. But I still hadn't forgiven Caleb for going behind my back to commit me. I still hadn't talked to him since he left me here. "This is the hardest thing I've ever done," he whispered as he hugged me goodbye.

"You're getting rid of me for who knows how long. I think it's the easiest thing. Now you can watch your fucking porn all night long and not worry about being interrupted. You can spend time with the boys without worrying about my annoying any of you. You're shipping me off when all I need is just your support. I can get better if you help me."

"I'm going to ignore everything you're saying, Kate. I know you're just upset. Someday, you'll thank me."

"I doubt that. I can't believe you didn't even let the boys come with us here. Don't you think I wanted every last minute with them? And I'll probably miss sixth grade graduation. I'm missing baseball games and the family picnic. It's not fair." I swallowed a sob and turned away. "Just go."

Caleb tried to hug me, but I twisted away. I still don't know if I've forgiven him, but I'm working on it in therapy. I may have forgiven him for leaving me here, because my therapist insists that it was a sign of love. But I don't know if I've forgiven him for not choosing somewhere that he and the boys could visit me. All the other women have people come, even Rose. My parents have come once. It's not easy for them to drive over three hours round-trip, and my mom calls during every visiting time and apologizes for not being there. My sisters, Jamie and Laura, have come twice. They cried and hugged me and promised to visit again as soon as possible. But everyone has their own lives. If I wanted to disappear, I feel like I'm doing a pretty good job.

"Weigh-in time!" The nurse's voice is too chipper as she calls us into her office one by one. *Morning Mantra* is followed by weigh-in three days a week. We are not allowed to look at the scale when we're weighed, so I turn my back to it and sigh. I don't even bother trying to explain anymore that I can see my weight...that putting on weight would thrill me, not freak me out.

"Good job, Kate." The nurse gives me a thumbs-up as she taps my weight into her iPad.

This is the first time I've had hope.

"Do you think I can leave today?"

"You know I don't make those decisions." She shrugs her shoulders. "Talk to your therapist. And I'm sorry to tell you this, but you never find out that you're leaving on the day you leave. There are a lot of things to get into place—a step-down program where you live, for one. You need to have someone come pick you up. We don't just push you out the door. Here at Serenity Cove, your continued success is as important as your success in the program."

I feel like telling her to shut it—she doesn't need to sell me on the program. I'll only like it when I'm looking back on it, instead of into it. Maybe.

Breakfast is fresh fruit, a mozzarella and spinach omelet and a giant egg bagel with butter. Rose eats about a third of everything and stands up. A peer counselor gently guides her back into her seat. "A bit more, Rose, or you'll need to make it up with the drink."

Rose grimaces and silently sits. I keep eating until my plate is clean. Whenever we don't finish our meal, we have "the drink." The amount we need to drink depends on how much of our meal we leave over. Two-thirds of the meal means that Rose will need to drink two bottles. Yes, they pour those bottles into the gorgeous crystal challises, but they still taste overly artificially sweetened with the texture of heavy cream. Not an easy thing to get down.

I look Rose right in the eyes. "You can do this, Rose. You can eat one more bite. And maybe that can turn into two."

She looks terrified but takes another bite. And then one more. "I can't. I can't eat any more. I'm sorry, Kate."

"You don't need to apologize to me. Those two bites are a victory. I know that. And now you have a little less to drink."

"A few sips, but yeah. Thank you." Rose squeezes my arm.

Our peer counselor, Rebecca, turns to me, "Thank you, Kate. You helped Rose a lot. That's what Serenity Cove is all about. We help each other overcome."

In my therapy session, my social worker, Julia, hands me a box of tissues. "We're going to dive deep today into your reasons for not eating. I know you told me you don't care about being skinny, which is why most of the women are here. Controlling their weight is a way to control their lives." She pauses, gazing at me, so I nod.

"It's about so much more than looking good. Does any of that resonate with you? Are you trying to wrestle control of your life?"

"Maybe. I don't know. I just get a lot of stomachaches and have since a…" I pause, not sure how to continue.

"Go on…"

I take a deep breath. "Since a violent incident in college."

"This is progress. This is the first time you're naming the enemy of your eating healthy."

Another catchphrase...the enemy of eating. I wonder if the therapists at Serenity Cove receive a list of phrases to employ in sessions. They are all impeccably dressed, perfect glossy hair, and seemingly right out of social work school. Sometimes it feels awkward spilling my guts to someone probably fifteen years my junior, but spill I do...because I want to get out of here, and I know one of the benchmarks they look for is self-awareness of why you don't eat.

"Yes. The enemy was a violent incident when I was twenty. It wasn't right away, but eventually the stomach pains got to be too much, and I ate only the simplest of foods. I lost over fifteen pounds." I pause for a moment and then add, "I was better for a long time, though. I gained enough weight to have two healthy pregnancies. I just went along with my life. So, I know I can get better again. I did it before."

"What changed that brought the eating disorder back?"

"I don't know if I'd call it an eating disorder. I just kind of lost my appetite."

"How much weight have you lost since you lost your appetite?"

"I don't know; they won't let me see my weight."

"Okay, how much did you lose before you ended up here?"

"I don't know...I'd say ten pounds at the most."

Julia picks up her iPad and clicks a few times then scrolls until she says, "Ah, here it is. Your medical records when you were admitted stretched back to your last physical five months ago. According to that, you lost twelve pounds between then and the day you were admitted here."

I ignore the number and ask a more important question. "Have I gained since?"

"I'm not supposed to tell you that, but since you insist you *want* to gain weight, and maybe some success will spur you on, yes, you've gained some weight back. But it's about more than gaining weight."

I don't even care what Julia is about to say, I know the spiel. I'm just happy I gained. One step closer to getting out of this place.

"It's about keeping the weight on when you leave, because you've confronted and overcome the demons that caused you to stop eating in the first place. Honestly, it's not that hard to gain weight when someone is standing over you making you eat."

"It's hard for the other women here. I see that. I eat more than everyone else at every meal. That has to count for something."

"It does, but it doesn't fix anything, especially if when you get home and no one is holding you accountable, you slip back. So, tell me about this violent incident."

I have a decision to make… I can deflect. I can make something up. Or I can tell her every horrendous detail, right down to facing the corner of the metal bathroom stall while Vin urinated inches away, while I tried to figure out how to escape.

"Okay…I had been drinking. But that didn't make me a victim, violence did…" The story unfolds with surprising ease once I get going. It's actually kind of cathartic, and I do the one thing I could never do in therapy in college. I cry.

"What sparked this rising up to the surface again? Not that pushing things down is a good thing, because it will always find its way back up…"

"I saw Vin Merdone, my attacker, on Facebook as someone I may know. I saw that my best friend who was always there for me—I fell in love with him for that, but never had the courage to act on it—was friends with him. I asked him to unfriend him, and he did right away. But then I became obsessed."

"Obsessed how?"

"I was convinced that he killed my friend. The murder was pinned on someone who confessed in a suicide note, but all those amateur detective boards in the underbelly of the Internet think he didn't do it."

"How did you end up on those? Were you obsessed with this murder, too, even before seeing your attacker?"

"No, but when I saw him…" I let out a long sigh. "Well, I started thinking about what other crimes he may have committed, because I only filed an anonymous police report, so he wasn't arrested." I shake my head. "Everyone told me since I was drinking, *I* would have gotten dragged through the mud if I pressed charges."

I pause and dab at my eyes with a tissue. "But I always regretted not formally accusing him. And when I saw on Facebook that he's had this amazing life since… I just *cannot* believe he's a millionaire. A fucking multi-millionaire!" My hand flies over my mouth. "I'm sorry for the language."

"No problem. You're in a safe space to express yourself," Julia says softly.

"Thank you. I appreciate that." I'm surprised to find I mean it.

"You're welcome. Go on…"

"Well, I saw how he's never paid for his crimes—I was sure that I wasn't the only one he assaulted. In fact, I got confirmation of that from something a friend of his wrote on Facebook…"

Julia asks, "What do you mean, 'You got confirmation?'"

"Vin posted on Facebook that he thought a football player accused of assault was a 'piece of garbage.' That infuriated me. He's such a freaking hypocrite." I pause, not sure I want to admit what I did next. I'm not very proud of it, but I think it's important to share.

Julia seems confused for a moment. "How did you see his post? Are you Facebook friends with him?"

"No, no—never. I had blocked him. But then I unblocked him and scrolled through his posts more than once. I couldn't help it—it was like a car crash I couldn't look away from."

"So, did you engage with him? How did you get your confirmation?

"Um, I'm not sure how to explain this without looking a bit crazy… I created a fake Facebook account—Jane Doe—and commented on Vin's post that I know what he did in college. His friend commented after me that Vin was a 'fucked up drunk' and 'the past couldn't stay in the past.' And there's more…"

Julia nods, waiting for me to finish speaking.

"His friend wrote, 'they,' not 'she,' about the girls he assaulted. If I was the only one, he would have written 'she.' It confirmed what I already knew in my bones. There were others."

"Do you spend a lot of time on his Facebook? Because if you do, that's a good place to start to limit the power he still holds on you. You can't break free of the past if you're still seeing him, even online."

I know Julia is right—it's not good for me. I would break out in a sweat every time I put his name in the search bar, feel like vomiting every time I'd see his face. I know it kills me a little each time. That wasn't the point of my sharing what I did, though. I wonder if Julia heard what else I said—that there were other women he assaulted. That's why I can't give up on finding the truth, even when I'm better. But, instead of pointing that out, I just tell her, "I know that. I eventually blocked him."

"That's a good start. Did that help?"

"Maybe. I still Googled crimes that happened in the same area around the same time. That's how I came upon the theories about my friend's murder."

Julia nods again and says, "Go on," as she furiously scribbles notes. I'd love to see what she's writing, but I know I can't.

"I guess I became a little obsessed with figuring out what else he may have done. I'd do research on cold cases from that time. It even started getting in the way of work. And I found myself unblocking him again and going on his Facebook, scrolling through his photos, getting angrier and angrier." I shook my head. "His life seems perfect. He never paid for what he did."

"And is this why you stopped eating?"

"Yes. I'd get terrible stomachaches. The stress of seeing him again was ripping me to shreds. How could he have just gone on with his life? I became consumed with wanting to make him pay. But I couldn't figure out a way to do that."

"That's a very common desire for rape survivors—very normal. But when it consumes you, that's when you need to banish it and move on."

I sigh and look away from Julia. I can see the ocean out the window, and I suddenly have a desire to just walk into it. Everything feels so hard. But I've never been one to take the easy way out, so I turn back to her. "I can try. I know, the more wrapped up I became in my revenge fantasy, the more stomach pains I had and the more I lost my appetite."

Julia gazes at me for a moment and then nods. "I'm going to suggest something radical. You've given this traumatic experience too much power over you. What if you chose forgiveness?"

"I don't know if I can do that."

"Your forgiving this person who has hurt you so terribly does *not* mean that he hasn't done anything wrong. It just means that you're no longer imprisoned by his actions. It sets you free. Anger keeps you stuck in the same patterns. Forgiveness is the key that can open the prison gate. You're not doing it for him; you're doing it for you."

I had never thought of forgiveness as something I could do for myself. My hatred for Vin has burned inside me for decades. I didn't know if I could extinguish it so easily. "I'll think about it," I tell Julia as my session ends.

"Okay. But please remember one thing…if you want to get out of here quickly, forgiveness is the key ingredient to success. Once you let go of your anger and desire for revenge, you can start to heal your relationship with food."

Once I start thinking about forgiveness as something I do for myself, not for Vin, it gets easier to contemplate. I try to remember even one thing I saw on his Facebook profile that indicated that he's changed. There was a post about Alcoholics Anonymous and how he did their Twelve Steps and asked for forgiveness. It doesn't make what he did any better—he never apologized to Jane Doe, only threats, but it lets me feel like I'm off the hook a bit. I can let go of my boiling, searing anger if it will save my life and my family. There's someone else I need to forgive first.

"Can I talk to Dad?" I ask Jacob as we finish our nightly conversation. I only have ten minutes left before *Goodnight Gratitude*, our nightly walk in the moonlight to the sensory garden where we sit in front of a small flowing fountain filled with smooth rocks and list all the things we were thankful for that day. Most of us struggle with the answers, and our peer counselors gently suggest tiny victories, which we repeat, simply to get done quicker, whether we're grateful or not. But tonight I hope to be truly grateful.

When Caleb gets on the phone, I say two words, "I'm sorry."

I don't hear anything, so I repeat myself and then ask, "What, you don't forgive me?" That's when I hear the sharp intake of breath and the sob. I've never seen nor even heard Caleb cry—it sounds almost feral.

In the background I hear Oliver ask, "Are you okay, Dad?"

"I don't want you to be sorry," Caleb eventually says. "I just want you to get better."

"I'm trying."

"I know. I'm just grateful that you finally realized that I didn't do this to harm you. I want you to be alive for a long time, and the way you were going…" Caleb pauses, and I hear another strangled sob. "I was afraid you'd die."

"I'm not going to die. I just want to come home. I don't think I was in danger of dying, but I guess I can understand your fear. I'm sorry again that I've put you through this. I had to forgive you first before I could say sorry. I know that you did this with my best interests in mind, but I was still angry that you went behind my back. I'm an adult, and you didn't make me a part of the decision process."

"You would have never agreed to it. I knew if I could just get you in the door you would be more likely to stay. And you know, you could have refused to stay…even when we got there. You could have walked out, but you didn't. That's when I knew it was the right thing to do, even if you were angry."

"I suppose that's true. But I still wish you hadn't told everyone else and kept it from me." I pause. "By the way, did you tell Sean about it? He usually texts me once or twice a week just to check in, but he hasn't at all since I've been here. I thought he would be worried about me."

"Um, okay…didn't realize Sean is so important to you that you miss hearing from him."

"It's not that, it's just weird, that's all."

"I did actually tell him not to contact you. I found him on Facebook and sent him a message. Since you're our mutual friend, it was easy."

"Why?"

"I just thought the less distractions, the better. And Sean is a distraction. You can escape into hours-long texting sessions with him and ignore that everything is collapsing around you. I know he's your crutch and has been since before we met. I'm not an idiot. Hold on."

I wait while it sounds like Caleb is moving. I hear a door close.

"Okay, I wanted to go in the basement where the boys wouldn't hear me. You say I escape into porn late at night. But how do you think I feel when you text with Sean? It's like the boys go to sleep, and you grab your phone and disappear, even if you're right there. Do you think I don't realize whom you're messaging with? Your face lights up when you get a text from him. It never lights up like that for me."

I don't know what to say, so I'm silent.

Caleb continues, "We both escape. At least there's no personal connection with mine."

"But you're watching other women naked," I whisper. "That's far more intimate than a text, even if you don't know them. Sean and I have never exchanged anything more than words."

"Yeah, and those can be way more powerful."

"Look, I'm sorry I brought it up. I don't have much time. I just want to say that I forgive you, and I hope you'll forgive me."

"You're forgiven," Caleb says, but it's drowned out by an overly chipper, "It's *Goodnight Gratitude* time, ladies! Come down to the Milieu room!" coming over the intercom system into my room.

"I have to go. I need to hand in my phone and go to the stupid garden to say what I'm thankful for tonight." I had thought I would have more to be grateful for, but now that I know how Caleb feels about Sean, I'm not so sure. I never knew our relationship bothered him. And then I start to wonder if he welcomed the opportunity to tell Sean not to contact me. I know I'm being paranoid. And the fact that I'm bothered by what Caleb did probably proves that he was right to do it. I never really considered the ramifications of our relationship on my marriage.

In the serenity garden I take the smooth stone that's passed from person to person and wait a moment before speaking. Until now I've only said what I think they want to hear. *I'm grateful for insight into my food issues. I'm grateful to have conquered a meal.* But tonight I want to mean what I say. Something feels like it shifted in me, and I need to acknowledge that. "I'm grateful that Julia opened my eyes to the power of forgiveness. The first person I forgave was my husband for making me come here. I'm sorry, but I was so angry at him when he drove me here and walked out the door. I know he did it to help me. And I've forgiven him in my heart for not visiting. I know we live five hours away and our kids are in school, but I thought he could come for a weekend."

Rebecca rubs my shoulder. "Is there anyone else you're thinking of forgiving?"

I'm guessing Julia shared notes from our session, and she's asking about Vin. We were told early on that the social workers and peer counselors discuss our cases in order to make for seamless treatment, since the social workers only see us three times a week, and the peer counselors live with us twenty-four hours a day. "Maybe."

"That's a start."

I pass the stone to Rose. As she takes it, I notice the skin on her hands is almost translucent in the moonlight. I can see every vein. "I'm grateful for..." She pauses, searching for the words when there are none. She's slipping away. "I'm grateful for Kate." She turns and smiles at me, and for that moment I can see her incandescent beauty.

"I'm grateful for you too, Rose." I lean over and hug her. She smells like a vanilla cupcake, and I find myself wondering if she wears that scent to remind her of what she won't eat anymore. That feels impossibly sad.

At sunrise the next morning I'm awoken by paramedics barging into my room instead of by Rebecca like I usually am. They begin furiously working on Rose as Rebecca stands back crying. I jump out of bed. "What's going on? What happened to Rose?"

Rebecca is crying harder as they use the AED on Rose. We watch as her body raises up and drops, motionless. Rebecca manages to get out, "I don't know. She wouldn't wake up. I shook her, but she's unresponsive. I could feel her pulse, but it's weak. I ran out and called 911. I didn't have my cell, so I had to run down the hall to the landline." So that we don't feel resentful, the staff locks their cell phones up every morning, as well. "No medical is here yet. Oh my God. Did you notice anything last night when you went to bed?"

"No. Nothing out of the ordinary. I was shocked waking up to this." I start to cry, too.

"I didn't even think to wake you up. I'm sorry you woke up to this."

"I only care that Rose is okay. I've only known her for two weeks, but…" I can't even finish.

"I know," Rebecca whispers. There's a certain bond between people battling an eating disorder. It's so hard to understand from the outside that when you meet someone who gets it, you've found a life-long friend. The other women in the program keep mostly to themselves and are younger than Rose and me. And when you share a room with someone, you're in the trenches together all the time. I couldn't bear to see her slip away.

A paramedic lifts Rose onto a stretcher. It seems like he's lifting a feather. "I'm sorry. There's nothing else we can do. Is there a next of kin you can call?"

"Oh my God, oh my God, oh my God" I just keep saying it over and over again. "What happened?"

The paramedic shakes his head sadly. "Probably cardiac arrest from anorexia. We see it a lot in these cases. You can be in treatment, but all the past damage is done. If you don't eat enough, your body eats your heart." He looks right at me when he says this. "It needs to consume muscle for energy if you don't give it enough fuel. And your heart is a muscle."

We skip *Morning Mantra*. It's not possible with Rose's death hanging over us. Schedule is the biggest part of Serenity Cove. We keep to a strict schedule no matter what—regimented meals and activities at the same time every day. But not today...today we simply sit in what they call the Milieu room, because every room has a name, on the sumptuously deep chocolate velvet sectional that takes up much of the space. Rebecca speaks first. "This has never happened at Serenity Cove in the three years we've been here."

"That's not that long," whispers the young woman to my left, Jess. She's about twenty-two or twenty-three and isn't yet showing the ravages of the disease, though she is extremely thin.

"You're right," Rebecca acknowledges. "But we are usually quite good with identifying those in the danger zone, health-wise, and getting them to the hospital. Obviously, we deal with one of the most gravely ill eating disorder populations. In-patient is the next step after residential, so there's always the chance of tragedy, but this was unexpected. Rose seemed okay last night. She drank all of her nutritional supplement to make up for what she didn't eat at dinner."

"Yeah, but when did the doctor see her last?" Jess challenges. "I think it's been four days for me."

"You're more stable. The doctor saw her two days ago. She had some chest pain, but he did an EKG, and she was fine."

"You better hope her family doesn't sue the shit out of you." Jess swings her glossy chestnut mane back over her shoulder and rolls her eyes. "I need to get the fuck out of here before you kill me, too."

Rebecca protests, "We didn't kill her. She was very, very ill." She pauses. "You'll all see your social workers today for an extra session, even if you weren't scheduled. We are here to support you."

In the instant that Rose's lifeless body was carried out of the room, I made a decision. This would be my last week in this place. Starving myself is not an option anymore. If forgiving Vin is the only way to repair my relationship with food, since it was first fractured in the aftermath of his assault, well, I'd just have to forgive him.

My session with Julia starts moments later. The tears flow as soon as I sit on the overstuffed olive chenille loveseat across from her black leather club chair. She hands me the box of tissues.

"I know it's so hard to lose Rose like we did. Not only did you lose a friend, but it forces you to confront your own mortality with this disease."

"I don't want to die," I croak through tears.

"Remember, it's in your power to live and live fully. It's a tough disease, a horrendous disease, and even when you're in remission, it can creep back in. You're always on the journey. That's why here at Serenity Cove we make sure you have a plan in place before you leave."

"I just want to leave. I'm okay. I'm not going to starve myself again. I'm not. I forgive Vin. He has no power over me. I don't care that his life went on without any consequences." I'm an ugly crier, and I know that I look horrible right now. It doesn't matter, I just continue through the tears. "Please just let me leave. I want to get home to my family. I miss my boys. I miss being a part of life. I had checked out from my life before I got here—all I could think about was Vin. But now that I know what it's like to really miss out, I won't ever do that again. Please." The sobs are racking my body.

"I understand. And I'm very happy that you've decided to forgive Vin. That's a huge step. But I don't make the decision alone about when you can leave. The medical director has to weigh in. Your nutritionist. The psychiatrist. We all make a joint decision. Let's see how you do with your meals going forward and what you weigh over the next week."

"Week? No, I can't wait another week. It's been two, but it feels like forever."

"Just keep moving forward and eating. As the weight goes up, you'll feel better and be able to eat more. As tragic as losing Rose is, it just may have sped up your recovery significantly, if you use this horrible situation as impetus to live in a healthier way." Julia nods sagely, and I want to smack her, which shocks and embarrasses me.

"Okay."

We spend the rest of our session figuring out my post-treatment plans, which I take as a good sign. I'm still racked by grief and panic. But I'd rather feel that way at home. At lunch and dinner, I eat everything. I even eat my entire late-night snack—I haven't had to have a liquid supplement in two days. At bedtime I just sit and stare at Rose's bed, the shockwaves of watching her die coursing through me again. I'm changed forever.

Since there are only five of us now and eight bedrooms, I ask if I can switch into one of the empty rooms that haven't even been used since I arrived. That day I was told that two women are in each room, because at Serenity Cove they feel that it's easier to triumph over this disease when you're not alone…at all. But now I want to be alone. I need to be alone.

Luckily, the peer counselor on call tonight, Tori, is understanding and lets me switch into one of the biggest rooms, one with a cozy window seat overlooking the garden. It's still not home, but it's better than my last room. And death doesn't hang in it. In that still moment, gazing over the garden, I feel incredibly grateful to be alive. I'm also grateful to get a second chance. And I swear to myself that I will make the most of it. The next week goes by in a blur of therapy and yoga and meals that I finish. I still feel Rose's absence acutely, but it propels me to do more. At my three-week mark weigh in, I've gained six pounds. Two pounds a week. That's the maximum you can gain because the nutritionists increase your food slowly so your system isn't shocked. You don't enter an eating disorder program to gain ten pounds in a week or two. You enter to change incrementally, to change your life going forward.

"Okay, Kate…" Julia begins as I sit down across from her for my session a few hours after weigh-in. She pauses and smiles. I can't believe that she may say the words I've been waiting to hear since I stepped foot in Serenity Cove. I tap my foot in nervous anticipation. "You've got your discharge date. It's a week from today. I think letting you see your weight gain helped tremendously. You know how much you've gained, right?"

"Yes—six pounds. I never thought I'd reach that."

"You did, thanks to your hard work. There's still a lot more work to do. You should gain at least six more, but ideally ten to fifteen. Even before you started losing weight a few months ago, you were a little underweight. If you gain six, you'll just get back to where you were."

"I understand. I know I can gain ten. Once I'm home with my family, I'll eat more. I promise."

"I know you'll try your hardest, but you know you'll also need a strong support program in place.

I nod in agreement. Whatever Julia says, I'll agree with.

"Great. You'll do step-down in your town, we already called the program there to set it up, and they accepted you. It's three nights a week for three hours each time. It's essential you do this for at least three months."

"Thank you so much, Julia. I will absolutely do it for three months. As long as I'm home, I can handle it."

"I also need you to remember something, Kate. Recovery from an eating disorder is a lifelong journey. You may have setbacks along the way, but don't let that discourage you. It's always lurking around the corner, but now that you have a toolbox to deal with it when it rears its ugly head, you can beat it. Just be aware of danger points."

"Danger points?"

"If you feel vulnerable or even just not in control, you might use food as a proxy to gain control over something. Just keep that in mind. Maybe jot it in your treatment diary."

I picked up the leather-bound notebook I was given at my first session—Serenity Cove spares no expense for their clients—and open it to the first blank page. I've filled up about two-thirds of it, and by the time I leave, it will probably be close to full. I inscribe Julia's advice. And then I add, "Recurrence is not failure. If you beat this once, you can beat it again. Failure is not an option. Always remember Rose."

PART TWO

CHAPTER SIX

April 2019

I RUN MY hand over the impossibly smooth leather-bound journal before cracking it open. It's almost five years old now. It's replaced my well-worn flowered journal from college as my reading material on April fifteenth every year. I prefer to revisit my triumphant moments, rather than the worst night of my life. I reread those last pages that chronicled my discharge, especially the part about recovery being a lifelong journey and the words, "Recurrence is not failure…" It's hard to remember that sometimes.

I've had my ups and downs, but I felt free after forgiving Vin, really free. I blocked him on Facebook, so I wouldn't even be tempted to see his unfettered life. And from the moment I returned from Serenity Cove, things were better between me and Caleb than they had been in years. The night I got home we sat on the couch after the boys were asleep. Caleb's arms were around me, his cheek resting against my hair. He spoke quietly, "You know, contrary to what you thought while you were away, I was devastated the whole time you were gone, missing you desperately. And I have a new appreciation for how hard you work just being a mom."

"Thank you. That means a lot." I leaned over to kiss Caleb, melting into him. For the first time in months, I felt desire creeping back in. As he lifted me up and carried me upstairs, I knew things would be okay. And they were for a long time. But then…then I heard a candidate for president brag about grabbing pussies, and no one seemed to care. The day after the election I cried for hours. The worst part was the argument I had with Sean.

"Why are you so angry about this?" he asked me when I railed about Donald Trump's Access Hollywood tape.

"How are you not angry? You're a detective for God's sake…in the sex crimes unit."

"Yeah, but he supports cops. And that's important to me. You'll see…he'll be okay."

It felt like a slap in the face that Sean didn't care one bit about all the assault accusations against his candidate. I cried as much for that as I did about a sexual predator being elected to the highest office in the land. But it didn't derail my eating. I moved on, because I had to…because I remembered Rose and decided to choose to keep eating, even when I didn't feel like it.

And now twenty-six years later, I feel at peace on this day. It's not completely easy, of course. I still remember every detail, but forgiveness leaves you with a lightness. It makes you feel a bit like you're watching someone else's movie. You can remember all the bad things that happened, but they don't cut through you as much.

In fact, now that our kids are big—fifteen and seventeen, Caleb doesn't take them out anymore, of course. Instead, I read my Serenity Cove journal, and then we go out to dinner to celebrate my triumph over the past. Tonight, I choose a little Italian place that we love and feast on baked ziti, garlic bread and tiramisu for dessert. Falling asleep that night, I feel sated and content. Five years since one of the darkest moments of my life, I know I can tackle anything thrown my way.

The next afternoon that feeling dissipates when I click on Twitter and see "Vin Merdone" trending. After the initial shock of seeing his name in a way I never in a million years expected, I have a tiny frisson of excitement that perhaps he was caught for some horrific crime and would finally see justice coming to him. Karma had finally caught up, I was sure. But when I click on the hashtag it's far worse than I could ever have imagined. The Twitter moment reads, "Multi-millionaire tech entrepreneur, Vin Merdone, has joined the Democratic presidential race. Merdone made his fortune in technology and created an app for those battling addiction. Merdone has been open about his past battles with addiction and believes he can solve the opioid crisis."

I throw my phone. "This can't be happening," I whisper as the veil of my sanity is ripped away, exposing the raw wounds I've buried so carefully. My phone chimes from across the room with a text. I slowly stand up and retrieve it. It's shattered, but when I peel off the glass screen protector, spider-webbing it more, the surface beneath it is smooth. I marvel at how that one impossibly thin buffer kept my phone from shattering and wish I had something like that around me.

The text is from Sean. *Did you see about Vin?*

I text simply, *Yes.*

You okay?

I don't know.

You won't vote for him, will you? You always say anyone is better than Trump, but the guy who raped you?

I put my phone down. I hate the word rape. I use assault. I don't like to be reminded of what it really was. Or even better, I prefer my college choice, "the incident." Sean knows this, and I wonder if he's specifically pushing my buttons, getting a reaction out of me.

I answer, *Of course not. I won't vote for him in the primary, and hopefully it won't go further than that.*

What if it does?

I don't want to think about that possibility. I haven't even answered before his next text comes in: *He's already got a ton of attention and fundraising. He's positioning himself as the Dem Trump…troubled past. Tells it like it is. Brash and uncouth. The real Dems won't go for it, but those who voted for Trump as an outsider but can't stomach his racism may in droves. People are saying he's the kind of guy you could have a beer with.*

I stand up and look in the mirror over my dresser. I see the change in my face already, it's drawn and pale. This was the last thing I ever expected, and I don't know how to navigate it. When the "Me Too" movement first surged up and caught powerful men in its net, holding them accountable for years of horrendous behavior, I wondered if maybe forgiveness wasn't the right path. I wondered if maybe the righteous anger so many were feeling would propel me to speak my truth. Then I felt a bit defeated, because all of the women coming forward were taking down men in the public eye. Who would care if I came forward about Vin? Sure, he was a millionaire, but until now he was an unknown millionaire. Maybe if he were a billionaire, more people would have known him.

I was almost envious of the women coming forward to bring down powerful men, which is kind of ridiculous—it's never easy standing up, it's never easy being brave and open. I felt like I was neither of those things. But I had my forgiveness, and I clutched it like a talisman. I was genuinely afraid that if I let myself feel the anger again, Vin would control me and everything I had accomplished would fall away.

Still, I wanted my chance to tell my story. I wanted it to matter. But it was safer knowing that no one would care— that I could just push it down and take it to my grave. I liked believing that the panacea of forgiveness would save me. Now…now people would care. I have my chance to tell my story and try to take my demon down. But I honestly don't know if I can.

I pick up my phone and type, considering each word carefully… *I can't think about him being successful right now. Maybe other women will come forward, since I was not the only one. The Dems wouldn't ever put up with a sexual assaulter on the ticket. Look at Al Franken, and what he did was a million times less than what Vin did to me.*

Before I can even figure out if Sean is pushing the issue because Vin is a threat to Trump, or because he wants me to feel empowered to speak my truth, my phone chimes. *Why don't you bring him down?*

I pause for a moment, but the answer is clear. *Me? I don't think so. Not right now. I don't want him to see me.*

Within seconds, it chimes again. I marvel for a brief moment at how fast Sean types, but then I realize that he probably had it teed up. I could see the little dots indicating he was typing before I even hit send. *I'll help. I think we gave up too soon last time. You went for treatment, and I didn't want to bring it up when you got back. I didn't want to tell you the leads I found, because I thought then you'd relive it. You said you forgave him and moved on. I figured it was better left in the past. Plus, you seemed so fragile. I think you're stronger now. I know you're stronger now.*

I write back quickly, *Leads???? Why the hell didn't you tell me? Isn't part of the protect and serve oath that if you get damning information on someone, you have to bring him in for questioning or something?* I don't know how he could have kept this from me.

Here's the thing, Vin is VERY well-connected, both in FL and MA. I did show the chief what I found, but he said that was all a long time ago, and it doesn't matter now. Vin turned his life around.

I 'm not sure if I even want to know, but still I type, *What did you find?*

My heart hammers in my chest as I wait for Sean's reply. *There were three other anonymous sexual assault reports and one closed discipline case from the college that I assume was the same thing. He was also arrested in a bar fight and then arrested for domestic violence a couple of months later. He punched his girlfriend in the head during a fight, but she declined to press charges, so the case was dropped. And...get this...he was at the mall the night Gina was killed. An eyewitness saw them arguing, but then couldn't remember if she saw him walk out after her. And then she recanted her story completely. Police never pursued it since she was an unreliable witness. And then Albert Jones very conveniently admitted to the murder before he killed himself. Why would they pursue anything else when they had a killer who was already dead? If Albert Jones hadn't confessed, I think Vin would have been a suspect and may have ended up behind bars back then. But by the time I dug all this up, no one cared, and if they did, they weren't going to upset their biggest benefactor.*

I'm dumbfounded and momentarily angry that Sean never told me this. But then I'm grateful. If I knew all this, I wouldn't have been able to forgive Vin. I wouldn't have been able to ascend from the ashes of my life through the grace of forgiveness if I knew for sure how evil he is. I need to just separate myself from this. I don't want to sink back into anger and hatred. I don't want to spiral down. I type, *I don't think I'll even need to say anything. Some intrepid journalist will dig all this up quickly, I'm sure. It will be done before he even gets going.* But the thought that someone placed him at the mall the night Gina was killed raises the hair on the back of my neck and leaves a pit in my stomach. I have to push this out of my head before I spiral again. I have to...the person recanted her story. Someone will surely find out the truth...if there's anything to find.

I see the little dots again indicating Sean is typing. Then they stop and start. I wait for what seems like a long time before my phone chimes again. *I wouldn't count on that. If you ask me, Vin greased some palms a long time ago to push stuff under the table. Got everything hidden real well. I found it as a detective in this precinct, but I don't know if anyone else would. I never thought this little college town would be so corrupt. He had just made his fortune around the time I was digging around and had paid for a new wing of jail cells. I think the chief tipped him off that I found stuff he might not want getting out. Vin said at the dedication that he spent time there in his early twenties for drugs and disorderly conduct and wanted to repay the fact that they straightened him out. Conveniently left out the sexual assault and domestic violence and the tip placing him at the scene of a murder. That kind of stuff doesn't fly well at events like that.*

I answer quickly. *You saw him five years ago???* That's all I took from that. I feel a little faint. I didn't even realize Vin was in this town. I thought he was far away in Florida. The fact that while I was unraveling, he was in my town—near my family—killed me.

Listen, Caleb asked me not to contact you. So, I didn't. Especially about that. It was while you were away, thankfully. The dedication was in the paper. I was happy you didn't see it.

I have to go, Sean.

Sean answers me anyway. *Please think about it. You have the power in your hands to bring the motherfucker down.*

Is this about Trump?

It's about us. He destroyed the possibility of us. He destroyed you, and now I want him to pay.

I'm trying to square this with the fact that when Vin first showed up on my Facebook, it was because Sean was friends with him. And he moved on with Nicole decades ago. He was over me then, but now he wants to make Vin pay for destroying us?

Okay, Sean. Have a good night.

Love you. Good night.

This is the first time in almost five years that Sean has signed off a text with *Love you*. I don't answer.

I'm at the stove cooking dinner when Caleb walks in the door. He circles one arm around me from behind, lifts my hair up with his other hand and kisses the back of my neck. "Mmm...smells delicious. Both you and the food. What are you making?"

"Just chicken cutlets. Nothing fancy. The boys will be home from baseball practice soon." It's still a little odd that once Jacob turned seventeen, I no longer needed to pick him up from sports practice, school, the mall...anywhere. And since he and Oliver are both on the varsity baseball team, I don't need to pick Oliver up after practice either. I really miss being chauffeur mom. Trapped in the car, I could usually get my boys to talk to me a little. Now, they'll come home, wolf down dinner and retreat to their rooms. It was odd getting used to full-blown teenagers, instead of needier kids. In fact, I still sometimes feel a little disoriented with the slowed-down rhythm of parenting older kids. But Caleb seems to be having a much easier adjustment. I suspect he'll handle an empty nest much better than I will.

"So, we're alone?" he asks, nuzzling my neck.

"For about ten minutes."

"That may be enough." Caleb grins wickedly. "I've been thinking about you all day. What do you say I give you a little oral treat? Put the chicken on simmer for a few. I can get you to have one in five minutes I bet."

The best part about treatment and gaining weight was my agreement with Caleb. I promised to not starve myself, and he promised to break his porn addiction. So far, at least to the best of my knowledge, he's kept his promise. It helped that I finally got my sex drive back. Forcing myself to forgive Vin was the most transformative thing I have ever done. Forgiveness frees you up. After I forgave Vin, it was easy to forgive Caleb for his lesser transgressions. He cried when I told him that I was past it.

It became addictive to forgive—I forgave every person for whom I had ever held a grudge and every person who pissed me off in daily encounters. From my nasty college statistics professor who told me that I was lucky that I was cute, since he was sure I'd never be successful to the dry cleaner who ruined my favorite dress to the guy who cut me off on the highway, and then flipped me the bird as he sped off. Everything rolled off my back. After Rose, I knew it was literally a matter of life and death to not be consumed by anger and resentment anymore.

But Vin running for president? That made me angry. Not just angry, but blood roiling furious. Steam coming out of the ears mad. Not able to even enjoy oral sex apoplectic. So, how could I hide this from Caleb?

"I'm sorry, it might *not* be that easy for me right now."

"Don't worry about dinner…time's ticking. If it burns, we'll order a pizza—the boys always want pizza."

"It's not that. Have you seen any news about presidential candidates today?"

"Nope. Been working all day. Wasn't on my phone at all, except to answer some emails during lunch. What's up, and what does the election have to do with your oral pleasure? Just think about Trump losing to literally any of the Dems. That should put you in a good mood." Caleb chuckles and winks at me.

"Vin Merdone is running for president." Like ripping off a bandage—quick and clean.

"Vin Merdone?" Confusion registers on Caleb's face, and I realize that he has no idea whom I'm talking about and for some reason that pisses me off. Sean knew right away…but Sean was there when it happened, I tell myself. It's not Caleb's fault he forgot. I haven't mentioned him in almost five years.

"The guy who assaulted me in college. He declared his candidacy today…as a Dem. It's trending on Twitter. He's positioning himself as a Trump-type candidate…for those who hate Trump, but also hate the establishment. Or for those who like some things about Trump but hate the racism and rhetoric."

"What. The. Fuck?"

"I know."

Caleb pulls me to him in a tight embrace. "I'm so sorry. You've come so far. You can't let this bring you down. Just ignore it. Seriously, who would vote for some unknown asshole."

"Remember—he's a millionaire, a multi-millionaire. People love millionaires. They think they have some key to fixing everything because they know how to make money. And he's got that troubled past that people seem to love now. If the candidate has done crappy stuff and can be president, I guess they figure it gives them a pass, too. He's also running on the platform of being a former addict. Says he beat his habit, and he created an app to help addicts, so he can fix the opioid crisis too."

Caleb is silent for a moment and then shakes his head. "Still, I don't think he'll get traction. Maybe people will come forward saying he's a sexual predator. You know, 'Me Too.' Dems don't stand for that shit."

"Sean texted me that he wants me to be the one to take him down," I say into Caleb's chest.

He hears me loud and clear and lets his arms drop, stepping back. "He's still texting you? I thought you guys weren't close anymore." The hurt invades his features, before he adds, "Did you tell him about Vin first? You could have called me at work. I would have listened."

"No…no. I didn't tell him. He told me. He texted me first. But I knew already. I had just seen it on Twitter. I don't talk to him often at all. You know, we don't agree on too much now."

"I'm sure that's why he wants you to take Vin down. He's a threat to Trump. He's using you, Kate. I know he was always one of your best friends, but if he supports that misogynistic asshole, he can't be *that* good of a person."

I fell in love with Caleb all over again in 2016 during the election. While I was despondent about no one seeming to care that Donald Trump was caught on tape admitting that he's a "pussy-grabber" and boasting that women let him do whatever he wants because he's a "star," Caleb became determined. He was horrified, indignant, furious. "Seeing what you've gone through even decades after being assaulted makes me understand the gravity of the situation," he shared with me one night not long after the tape was leaked. "So, I've decided that someone who thinks it's okay to assault women can never be our president. I'm going to try to keep that from happening by making phone calls for Hillary." He was true to his word and was a complete contrast to Sean.

It was a horrible time for sexual assault survivors but having Caleb work so hard to keep a predator out made me feel safer—protected. After the argument I had with Sean over Trump, I distanced myself. Honestly, I couldn't help it—it was for my sanity. I didn't unfriend him; I answered any messages from him; I even liked Facebook posts. But…I felt betrayed. I felt like it was a slap in the face that he could look past Trump's boasting.

I didn't even care about our different politics—we hadn't agreed on other candidates before, and our bond stayed as strong as ever. It wasn't about Republican or Democrat…it was about the fact that he could look the other way and give a pass to an admitted sexual predator who was accused by more women than I could count at that point, because in Sean's opinion, he "supports cops."

"I don't get his support of him," I admit. "And honestly you should be happy because it makes me appreciate you even more. But I do think that as a detective this is eating at him."

Caleb almost imperceptibly shakes his head.

"He said there was evidence that Vin was at the mall the night my friend, Gina, was killed, but his chief made him bury it. He found out while I was at Serenity Cove. He said he didn't want to interfere with my recovery by telling me about it when nothing would ever be done about it. He thought it would hurt me more to have justice not served. But now it's my chance."

"I think you need to be careful. Like I said, he could just be using you. How do you know it's real evidence? It seems a little too convenient."

I know it's entirely possible that Caleb is right, but I feel like a freight train that has left the station and can't be stopped now. The next morning, I text Sean to send me what he has on Vin. His reply is immediate. *I can't just send it to you. It's evidence. Even hidden evidence has to be handled properly. Just believe me.*

I'm going to need to see something solid before I come forward. Sorry. I pace my kitchen, waiting for Sean's reply.

But you don't even need the murder to come forward. He raped you.

I cringe. *Please stop using that word. Say assaulted.*

If you can't use the word, then I don't think you can come forward. That was unexpected. I put the phone down. I truly don't know what to say. I'm not hungry, but I toast a bagel, spread it with cream cheese and pour myself a glass of orange juice. I force myself to eat...one bite at a time, until it's gone. One thing I learned in residential, and that I've always kept in mind, is that once you eat less, it's easier to eat less. Your stomach shrinks and your hunger signals disappear. Your body gives up trying to tell you when to eat. If I keep eating, I hope I'll keep feeling hungry. Remission is not the same as cured. I never forget that.

Just as I'm about to step in the shower my phone chimes with a text from Sean. I read it as the bathroom steams up. *Look, I'm sorry. I don't mean to push you. You need to do what you feel comfortable with but remember he's a bad guy. He's just as bad as Trump, maybe worse, because he may have killed someone.*

I know I shouldn't escalate this, but I can't help it. *Just remember Trump raped a thirteen-year-old girl. Vin is horrible, but Trump is just as bad. Is this all about protecting Trump? Because if it is, I'm not interested in being a part of it. Come forward yourself.*

I step into the hot shower and let it run over me until my skin turns red. I spin back to the days after Vin attacked me when I'd take the hottest showers I could stand, hoping to wash him off of me. When I step out there's a text from Sean. I get dressed and towel-dry my hair before I sit down on the couch to read it.

I'm sorry. And it's not about Trump. I don't think he's perfect. If a better candidate came along, I'd vote for him or her. But Vin isn't it and you have the power to stop him.

I put my phone down and flip on the television. I never watch TV during the day, but I need a distraction. Work has crawled to a stand-still, and an undistracted mind is dangerous, I've learned. I started my own consulting business a little over a year after I returned from residential. My old boss, Virginia, kept her word and held my job, but then she left our company a year later. My new boss and I had friction from the start. He never overtly harassed me, but I could feel his eyes linger on me every time I walked by him. He'd wink at me and ask me to fetch him coffee. He clapped Caleb on the back when he met him and said, "You've got quite a girl there. Lucky man." Wink, wink.

Caleb didn't see anything wrong with it, and maybe there wasn't, but it just left me feeling a low level of the "heebie jeebies" all the time. Maybe if he were a grandfatherly type, I'd say it was generational, but he was my age. Luckily, Caleb fully supported my decision to strike out on my own since he had gotten a promotion and we didn't need my income anymore. The business was more for my sanity than for income. But being in a small town, it's not like there's a lot of room for two companies doing market research locally, and finding clients online was challenging. I turned to event planning on a much smaller scale—kids' birthdays mostly, the occasional Bar Mitzvah or wedding. It wasn't that big of a leap...planning A Taste of Rolling Green was just like planning one huge-scale party. And A Taste of Rolling Green went off without a hitch. At least that's what I was told—I was still at Serenity Cove that weekend, which broke my heart right along with every other soul-crushing thing about being there.

So, I knew I could plan a party. And I did pretty well for a while. I liked doing weddings—full of hope for the future. I found the venues and coordinated photographers, caterers, florists, a band or DJ...everything needed to celebrate love. But those were few and far between. Millennial brides liked to do the research on their own, everything is at their fingertips online. Bar and bat mitzvahs had their pleasures, too—I came up with a theme and often created the invitations and favors myself, since I've always been crafty. I bought a top-notch printer and even a small heat press at the craft store to make t-shirts. But this isn't a very Jewish town...now, if I still lived on Long Island, I'd make a killing; small-town Massachusetts not so much. When the boys were in Hebrew school, their classes had less than ten kids. When I was growing up on Long Island, I went to Bar Mitzvahs every weekend it seemed in seventh grade and the first half of eighth. My boys went to maybe half a dozen each. So, I phased both of those parts of my business out.

Now I just focus on children's birthday parties, which are the most pure and joyous of the three, full of fun—the sole purpose to make little ones happy. I settled in there, finding my niche. But those have pretty much dried up, as well. I have a closet in my basement full of tiny toys—super balls; little green aliens; squishy baseballs; glittery purses sized for preschooler hands; stickers and pencils; and so much more. I think I started that business because aggressively focusing on moments of pure celebration kept me moving forward and helped me see more joy around me. It seems fitting that as I feel myself battling the descent back to the darkness, I haven't had the distraction of planning a happy event. I don't even have anything on the calendar.

So, I sit back and flip through channels, looking for something funny. Maybe *Friends* or *Seinfeld* reruns. *I Love Lucy* would be perfect. I remember I was always watching reruns of it when my dad would walk through the door from work right before dinner when I was a little girl. I watched reruns of it all night when I was in labor with Jacob. The hospital had sent me home right after I arrived at just after 1:00 am, telling me I was only three centimeters dilated and should labor at home and return in the morning. So, I spent the whole night in our cushy hunter green recliner, eating dry toast and watching *I Love Lucy*, dreaming about the baby I was about to meet.

I don't find *I Love Lucy*, but I land on something that makes my heart practically jump out of my chest. There's Vin on one of those local morning shows with overly blow-dried hosts, a man and a woman. She's blonde and wearing a coral wrap dress that highlights not only her golden tan, but her ample cleavage, as well. She laughs at something Vin says and touches his knee. They are all sitting on stools in a semi-circle. "So, Vin…do you mind if I call you Vin instead of Mr. Merdone?" she begins.

"Not at all," he answers with a wink. "I may be a candidate for president, but I'm just a regular guy."

I want to turn off the TV, but I can't.

"That *is* the appeal and thrust of your campaign, isn't it?" asks Blondie. I can't remember either of the hosts' names, even though I'm sure I watched this show years ago when my kids were younger. I'm not the type of person to sit and watch morning shows—I'd rather be out doing something or reading a book or really anything else. The insipid chatter gets to me. But now I'm glued to my seventy-two-inch flat screen that we got at a scratch and dent sale at the local appliance store last year. It feels like Vin is in my living room, invading my space.

"Yes," he answers quickly. "My campaign is about regular people getting represented. That was how Trump got elected—by claiming that he represented the little guy. But here's the thing. He's not a regular person. He's an out-of-touch, fake billionaire conman who made people believe that he's one of them. He views his supporters as suckers he can fool while taking their health care and destroying their quality of life by rolling back environmental regulations, waging a trade war with China that hurts our farmers or stealing from the military to build his useless wall."

Blondie nods her head in agreement, looking like she'd like to have Vin for lunch. "I'm not establishment. I'm not an elitist, and I'm not a far-left winger. I'm the candidate for all those disillusioned Trump voters." He smiles blindingly at the camera, and I wonder if he got his teeth whitened for the campaign. He has the perfect amount of stubble to make him look cool, but not Steve Bannon sloppy, and he's wearing a crisp white t-shirt, distressed—but perfectly creased—jeans and a leather motorcycle jacket. It's a nightmare. I have a sinking feeling that casual cool vibe will take him further than I initially thought.

The Ken doll looking co-anchor speaks for the first time. "You don't have any name-recognition, though. How will you get your message out there?" He seems a tad annoyed, maybe he and Blondie are having an affair and he's jealous. Maybe she's Barbie to his Ken.

Vin smiles self-deprecatingly before speaking. "Very good point, Steve." Okay, so his name is Steve. "But I actually have a huge platform on social media." There goes the self-deprecation. "My Instagram is filled with photos I've taken during my many motorcycle trips—people really connect with that. And I think they might like to live a bit vicariously, too—I've been to some ridiculously beautiful spots on my bike." He talks about it like it's a ten-speed. "I've biked through Europe and all across this great country, meeting amazing people along the way. That's what led me to run for president."

Barbie speaks up, "Your travels?"

"In a way...people know that I was a former addict. I always make that very clear, and it was the impetus behind my creating an app to match people battling drug addiction with those who have been there as coaches and mentors. Like a sponsor in AA, but more fluid than that."

I have no idea what he means by that—more fluid—but it's no doubt a good catchphrase. Barbie practically has drool hanging off her lip. "So interesting..."

"Thank you. So, when I post these amazing experiences, people tell me that I give them hope. That's what Obama gave people...hope. If I can give hope to those battling the most demons, you better believe I can give everyone who dreams of a better tomorrow, free from chaos and divisiveness, hope, too."

Barbie, gazing at Vin, "That is beautiful."

"He's fucking comparing himself to Obama?!" I practically yell at the TV. "Are you kidding me?" Now, I've heard enough and am about to switch it off and go throw in a load of laundry when Steve says something that stops me dead in my tracks.

"So, Vin—you'll be at Rolling Green College kicking off your campaign with a rally in two days, correct?"

"You got that right. I want to come back to where I started to embark on this amazing journey, which, win or lose, it will be an amazing journey. I was here during some of my darkest days. I had moments I'm not proud of, but in the end my time in jail here—yes, I was arrested for disorderly conduct and of course, drug possession—straightened me out."

"So brave of you to admit that to our audience here in Springfield and all of Western Massachusetts. Thank you, Vin," Barbie puts her hand on Vin's knee again.

"Wait, Brooke, there's something else I need to say…" So that's her name…Brooke. Well, I like it better than Barbie, and I guess it fits a gorgeous blonde.

"Yes, Vin?" Her luminous blue eyes never leave his face, and I wonder if she's married. I don't see a ring.

Vin looks right at the camera, his piercing dark eyes, almost black, welling with tears. "I'm sharing this here because I consider this area, especially Rolling Green, my home, no matter where I'm living, and I've lived a lot of places. It's where I grew the most. But it's also where I did things I'm the most ashamed of."

I put the remote down and sit, transfixed. It feels like Vin is staring right at me. I must be losing it. He rubs his eyes and sighs. "Okay, here goes… About five years ago, an anonymous person, Jane Doe was her Facebook name, commented on a public post I had put up deriding a football player for assaulting his girlfriend. She said that I assaulted her in college and called out what a hypocrite I was." Brooke gasps audibly. "And she was right. That comment has haunted me since. I didn't handle it in the best way. I still wasn't in a great place. I was suddenly very successful but felt empty inside. I had demons that I hadn't faced, even though I was sober. Her comment reminded me of that and terrified me."

Vin pulls an old fashioned, fancy handkerchief out of his pocket. I can see the beautiful cutwork embroidery as the camera zooms in on him, and he dabs his eyes. It seems like such a contrast to his tough guy image that I'm sure it only adds to his charm. "So, I forced myself to revisit some of the worst memories of my past, trying to unblock suppressed, traumatic memories in therapy."

Brooke seems to be over her shock and is leaning towards Vin, her hand on his arm now. Steve leans back, visibly skeptical, and I wonder if he's a Trump supporter or maybe a "Bernie Bro." He doesn't look like he's buying it, but Brooke is lapping it up. I would imagine that having a presidential candidate come on your local, small city morning show and drop a bombshell confession in your lap is not an ordinary occurrence. She puts her hand over her heart and sighs, tears welling in her eyes, too. Damn, she's good. If it wasn't about me, I'd say this is great television, especially for such a small market. "Go on," she says softly.

"That person accused me of something horrific, and my friend and lawyer basically corroborated her account, saying I didn't treat women very well in college…"

"Didn't treat women very well?!" I yell at the TV. "He agreed that you assaulted other women, not just me. He didn't say you just didn't call them after a date. *That's* not treating them well, you phony piece of shit." I sigh. He can't hear me. I really am losing it.

Vin stops to dab his eyes before continuing. "I lashed out at him and Jane Doe, and then deleted the post immediately. I had no recollection of ever mistreating anyone." Vin stares plaintively into the camera. "Here's the thing…when I was nineteen, twenty, twenty-one, I was high out of my mind every weekend at parties, at the bars. I managed to do well in school—I studied during the week, and figured I deserved to party on the weekends, so I didn't think I had a problem." Vin shakes his head ruefully. "But most Sunday mornings I'd wake up with no recollection of the night before." Brooke is transfixed, even with that admission.

Vin turns to her. "Have I gone over my time? I don't want to hog the whole show."

"No, no…we already bumped our next guest. This is more important. The owner of Picatso, a cat who paints, will be on tomorrow."

I would much, much rather be watching Picatso, but I can't bring myself to turn this off still.

Vin breathes an exaggerated sigh of relief. "Excellent. Thank you so much because what I'm sharing isn't just about me. There are legions of people out there stuck in the virtual prison of drug use, not to mention those who end up in actual prison. And not only do their actions affect themselves, but they affect everyone in their lives. People under the influence of drugs and alcohol hurt everyone one around them. Maybe not as much as I did, but they do…and they don't always mean to. I know I didn't. This is why we need to fix the addiction crisis." A dramatic pause… "You know, after college I didn't get better. I just got worse. Instead of being high only on the weekends, once I graduated, it was every day. I had moved home to my parents' house. I couldn't find a job with a journalism degree. I became depressed, and I drowned myself in more and more drugs until my parents kicked me out. I was homeless." Vin shakes his head mournfully. "Yup, I was out on the street. That makes me uniquely qualified to fix homelessness, as well as the addiction epidemic, because of course—they're two sides of the same coin. And sexual assault…all kinds of assault are right in the mix, too, when speaking about the effects of addiction."

Brooke sighs. "So true." Steve has been strangely quiet. I wonder if he has "Me Too" skeletons in his closet or if he just is seeing right through Vin's act. I'm assuming it's an act, because even though I forgave Vin, I did it for myself, not because I thought what he did was okay. Far from it. And I didn't forget. The viciousness with which he attacked me, the complete disregard for my fear, for my screams, was not due to addiction. It was due to evil. I know that in my bones. He can hide behind his excuse of being high as much as he wants, but I know the truth. He enjoyed what he did. It wasn't a question of misinterpreting my signals. He knew very well that I didn't "want it." If he thought I was a willing participant, he would not have dragged me to the bathroom so I couldn't escape. He was perfectly lucid, not matter what he says now.

He's droning on still. "I mean, if I could do the things I did…" Vin pulls out his handkerchief again and dabs at his eyes. "…just because I was high, well anyone can turn into a monster under the influence." Vin full on sobs, his shoulders shaking.

Brooke leans forward. "Are you okay? Do you need a minute?"

"No. No. I'm okay. I don't really have a right to cry over this, do I? Okay…" Vin breathes out heavily. "I want to own up to this. I support women. I support 'Me Too,' and I want to apologize to any person I've ever offended or wronged, especially Jane Doe, if she's out there somewhere."

Brooke gushes, "Amazing."

"Thank you. When I told my campaign manager about this, warning him that at least one woman might come forward with accusations, and possibly more, he said, 'Deny. Deny. Deny. You're a good guy, Vin. They'll believe you.'"

Vin shakes his head ruefully. "He said, 'Maybe not all the Dems, you know, look at Franken, but the Independents and the Repubs who are sick of Trump—they'll believe you. And if you have enough of their support, the Dems will vote for you in the primary, because you'll have the best chance of beating Trump.'"

Vin stares into the camera, silent for a moment. "I fired him."

Brooke gasps and applauds. Steve almost imperceptibly rolls his eyes at her. Maybe it's not that he doesn't buy Vin's bullshit. Maybe Steve is a Trump supporter...or maybe he *is* in love with Brooke and is jealous. It doesn't matter—I'm just glad that one of them isn't fawning all over Vin.

"Look, I'm no Donald Trump. I'm no Brett Kavanaugh. I don't need to deny. I believe women. I'm not the boy I was back then, treating my classmates disrespectfully."

Disrespectfully? Disrespectfully is not holding the door open for someone. Rape is violence, not simple disrespect. But of course, Brooke doesn't call Vin out on it. She's silent while he continues.

"I'm now a man who is willing to be held accountable. I'm a man asking for forgiveness and a second chance, because I can do so much good in this world. I know I can." Vin pauses. "In fact, I'm going to do some good right now. I'm going to put my money where my mouth is and make a $100,000 donation to RAINN."

Oh my God. He's fucking brilliant. He got ahead of any potential scandals and turned it around to show his altruistic side. Vin pulls out his phone and brings up the Rape, Abuse and Incest National Network website on his phone as the camera zooms in.

"Cool, I can use PayPal."

Brooke nearly falls off her chair fawning over Vin. "Oh, my goodness, Vin! That is so generous of you."

"Aww, it's nothing. It's the least I could do."

Anything I could possibly say now has lost its teeth. His donation will be easily verifiable, and I bet it will go viral. It's done. I click off the television. Forgiveness was a better path anyway. At least it benefits a good cause.

I grab my laptop, go on Facebook and click on the secret "Rolling Green Resistance" group I'm a member of, curious to see if anyone is talking about Vin. I don't know if it will be negative, because of what he admitted, or if he'll rope them in with his charm and donation to RAINN. Sure enough, there's already a post: *Okaaayyy... Long post alert... At first, I didn't give a second thought to Vin Merdone. I figured we don't need another outsider businessman. We need Elizabeth Warren or even Mayor Pete...love me some Mayor Pete. Or Kamala or Corey. Even Biden if he runs like they're saying he will, but he's not my first choice, because he's the old guard. So, I was set on supporting one of them. But damn, I'm willing to give Merdone another look. I mean it's horrible how he treated women, but if he owns up to it...we all did stupid things as kids. And at least he didn't rape a thirteen -year-old like Trump. Plus, he made that huge donation. And honestly, I think I'd vote for Elmo over Trump at this point. What do you all think?*

I snap my laptop shut and pick up my phone. *There's no point now. Whatever I say won't even make an impression...Vin beat me to it and made himself look like the good guy.*

Sean replies in seconds. *Why????? What happened??*

He was on Good Morning, Springfield, talking about how he'll be at Rolling Green for a rally, and he admitted that he sexually assaulted women in college while he was high, and then he made a $100,000 donation to RAINN, a rape awareness organization.

His reply is even quicker... *I know what RAINN is. That brilliant bastard. This will be harder than I thought. But we can take him down.*

I feel like Sean isn't comprehending what I'm saying, so I just put the phone down and go about my day. Tucking my horror as far down as it can go. I refuse, absolutely refuse, to go back to where I was five years ago. I can't. Forgiveness has worked so far. And now that Vin has apologized to me, or at least apologized to Jane Doe, which is the same thing, I will forget the violence again. It's the only way to live my life. I will forget the feeling of his hands pushing down on my shoulders. I will forget the evil glint in his eyes. I will forget the viciousness. I will forget that I know for certain that it wasn't just that he was high. I will forget. That's my new mantra, or maybe it's been my mantra for the past five years.

When Caleb comes home from work, I'm on the couch wrapped in a blanket with a heating pad around my neck. I'm simply staring into space. Jacob and Oliver are in their rooms, hopefully doing their homework, but just as likely they are wasting time on their phones…Snapchatting or watching YouTube videos. They will come out long enough to eat, and then scurry back in, like the shy hamster we had years ago who only ventured from his little purple plastic igloo house long enough to eat, drink and poop in the corner before hiding again.

I long for the time when I was intertwined in their lives, when I'd sit at the table with them helping them with homework or just discussing their days. It breaks my heart thinking that I missed such a huge chunk of that time five years ago. I was right in the thick of it in parenting back then—ten and twelve years old. My kids needed me, maybe not as much as when they were toddlers, but still they needed me, and I faded away. I still mourn that lost time. I can't get it back.

That's what I'm thinking about when Caleb flops down next to me on the couch. He pulls me to him and kisses the top of my head. I look up at him, and he brushes the hair off my face. It's such a tender gesture that I crack open, the tears spilling down my cheeks. "Hey, hey, what's wrong?" The concern is lacing his voice, but I don't want to dump on him.

"I'm okay...just feeling a little emotional. I was thinking about how the boys don't need me much anymore. Jacob will be going to college before we know it. And I thought about all the time I missed when they were little and still needed me." At this point, I'm ugly sobbing, and I don't know how to stop. I don't know how to stem this tide of feeling useless and bittersweet. I'm glad my boys are growing into amazing young men, but I wish I could get back the time I lost.

"First, you didn't lose that much time. What was it? Three weeks? A month?"

"I'm not only talking about the time I was away. I'm also talking about the time leading up to it, when I was so wrapped up with figuring out if Vin murdered Gina that I may have been present physically, but I wasn't really there." I shake my head. "And even when I gave up on that, I was eating so little that I was just in a constant fog."

"What's brought all this up? Is it what you told me about Vin running for president? I don't think it'll go anywhere. Just let it blow over."

"Caleb, he was on *Good Morning, Springfield* today. He's going to be kicking off his candidacy with a rally at the college in two days."

"Are you serious?"

"Yes. I wish I wasn't. He also brought up that he assaulted women in college, though of course he didn't say it as plainly as that. He said he 'mistreated' them when he was high. There's a huge difference between assault and mistreatment. Mistreating is not calling when you say you will."

"What an asshole."

"Yes, but here's the thing... He apologized. He owned it, and my hardcore liberal friends in the secret Facebook group I'm in fell for it hook, line and sinker."

"Wow. What's wrong with them?" Caleb shakes his head incredulously.

"Nothing. Vin seemed sincere, and as the person who posted about it wrote, she'd vote for 'Elmo' over Trump." I pause for a moment, trying to decide if I should tell Caleb about Jane Doe. I never admitted what I did. I figured it was a blip...I deleted the account right away, and no one had to know. Well, I told Sean, but that was it. But now it feels important that I share what Vin said. "He apologized directly to me. He said if I'm out there, he's sorry."

"What the fuck? He knows who you are? He knows your name? Are you okay with that? And how does he know? Is Sean behind this? Because I swear to God, I will fuck him up if he outed you."

"No, he doesn't know my name, and it had nothing to do with Sean."

Confusion invades Caleb's features. "Can you please just tell me what's going on? I can't help you if I'm in the dark."

I take a deep breath. "Okay, here goes... There's something I never told you. I created a fake Facebook account and confronted Vin on one of his posts five years ago."

"That doesn't seem safe at all, Kate. What were you thinking? He may have been able to figure out that it was you."

"He didn't figure anything out. I used the name Jane Doe and told him that he was a hypocrite, and I knew what he did in college. It was on a post he had put up about a football player who beat up his girlfriend or wife or something. He blasted the guy, and I just pointed out that he did the same or worse. He denied it and attacked me—said I better hope he never finds me, which made me literally get sick to my stomach. But then his lawyer, a guy we went to school with, corroborated my account and basically said there were multiple women, and that he would defend him if anyone came after his money or anything."

Caleb is staring at me, and I can't tell if he's impressed or horrified. "Wow, Kate. I don't know what to say," which still gives me no clue as to what he is thinking. "Why didn't you tell me about this?"

"I thought you'd think I was crazy."

"Look, I love you. I know you've been through something horrendous, and I think just surviving after it took a tremendous amount of courage. And I know that seeing him again on Facebook brought back all those demons. I'm sorry if I ever seemed like I didn't empathize and support you."

"Do you remember when Jacob said I'm crazy, and you whispered, 'If the shoe fits?'"

Caleb nods his head sadly.

"Well, that's how I felt all the time…like you thought I was crazy. So, I tried to hide much of it. But I can't do that anymore. I think being so isolated in my thoughts is what destroyed me last time." Caleb rubs my leg.

"I'm so sorry I was such an asshole. That's all I can say. You're the strongest person I know." Caleb pulls me to him in a hug and speaks into my hair. "So, Vin apologized to you as Jane Doe? And you're sure there's not another Jane Doe out there? A guy like Vin has probably left a ton of 'Jane Does' in his wake."

"It was definitely me he apologized to—he mentioned the post and my comment on it. He said that his friend reminded him of the awful things he had done, and he immediately deleted the post. But he decided to go into therapy to confront his demons. And he's a better person now. He used the excuse that he was high on drugs every weekend."

"Scumbag."

I pull away from Caleb and look him in the eye. "You have no idea. He knew exactly what he was doing when he assaulted me. And he knew it was wrong, otherwise he wouldn't have pulled me into the bathroom with him so I couldn't leave."

"How can this POS be running for president?" Caleb pauses. "What am I saying…look at Trump. It seems being a POS is an advantage. What is *wrong* with people?"

"So, what do I do? Sean wants me to bring him down, but he already admitted that he assaulted me. And he apologized. Do I continue on the path of forgiveness and just push away my horror? What if somehow he can beat Trump? Is that more important than my experience?"

"I don't know."

"What do you do when the bad guy is on your side? What do you do when he wants to save the environment, end the opioid epidemic, *get rid of Trump*?" I sigh and shake my head. It's a conundrum I never in a million years thought I would find myself in, and I don't know where to go from here. "I thought for sure Dems would never go for a sexual assaulter, and sure my little Facebook group is just a tiny microcosm of the general electorate, but man did he sound sincere. If I hadn't seen the violent glint in his eye…if I didn't have the bruises to prove what he did, I may have fallen for it too." The tears spill fresh over my lashes.

"I think you should stay on the path you've been on. You've been doing so great. Our boys have their mom back."

"They hardly need me anymore."

"They will always need you. You're their mom. It might not be with the same urgency that they needed you when they were little, and you had to wipe their noses and butts and help them with their homework and clean up skinned knees seemingly every day, but they still need you."

"Thanks, babe. You're right. I should just continue on the path I'm on, and hopefully karma will get Vin before his candidacy goes much farther."

My phone chimes with a text from Sean. *I have something I need to show you. Please answer me.*

I put the phone down and kiss Caleb long and soulfully, with everything in me.

CHAPTER SEVEN

BY THE NEXT morning Sean has texted me four more times. The last one says, *Look, I get that you've given up on making Vin pay. I watched the interview. It won't be easy. He's pretty fucking charming, isn't he? Fools everyone. But not me. I know what he did. And I have proof. People might look past sexual assault, but will they look past murder?*

"What the fuck?" I say out loud, I'm blindsided, but I guess I shouldn't be. Sean told me that evidence was buried. Sean told me that he thinks Vin murdered Gina, and it was all swept under the rug because they made an easy arrest. Albert Jones took the fall, and that's all they needed.

Caleb shoots up. "What's the matter?" he stammers, half asleep. I look at the time; it's only 6:30 a.m.

"Go back to sleep, hun. I'm sorry I woke you. I'll get the boys up." Caleb was right in one way that my boys still need me. I wake them up every day for school, make them breakfast and make their lunches. Caleb always tells me they're big enough to set an alarm and get up themselves, but I know it won't wake them. We tried that system, and they slept right through. Plus, I like getting up with them and feeding them. I like seeing them off to school. I only have one year left after this school year before Jacob graduates and goes off to college and three before Oliver does. Even if they stay local and go to Rolling Green, they both told me that they'll want to live on campus. The college has a special scholarship for local kids, so we could afford it. But I have a feeling that they'll want to escape our little college town.

I drag myself out of bed and pad into Jacob's room, then Oliver's. Both protest and roll back over. So, I need to resort to turning their lights on—not exactly nice, but necessary. And it gets them up, albeit not without more protests. The morning, as always, is a blur of microwaved pancakes drowned in butter and syrup, glasses of orange juice poured, and peanut butter and Nutella sandwiches slipped into baggies. Once I watch Jacob pull out of the driveway with Oliver yawning in the passenger seat next to him, I sit down to answer Sean.

It's over, I type. *Seriously, I just want to get on with my life and hope that he doesn't get the nomination. I really don't think he will.* I don't know how much I believe that, as the knot of fear tightens in my stomach. My eyes well up again. This is getting ridiculous, I'm not a crier. My breath quickens thinking about what evidence Sean might have and wondering if Vin might finally pay. I read about a cold case murder where new DNA evidence led to the arrest of a man who had also fondled women and forced them to perform oral sex. And I was jealous…jealous that these women would finally get to see their attacker face a reckoning twenty years later, even if it was for murder and not the exact crimes he committed against them. I want justice served. Forgiveness suddenly feels hollow as this torrent of emotion rushes through me.

Sean texts me, *Please, Kate. I don't want to text. There can't be a trail. I need to see you in person. That's all I can say.*

What the hell? *I'll think about it. I just need some time to process everything.*

I quickly put my phone face down on the counter as Caleb walks into the kitchen. "Do you want me to make you something for breakfast?" I ask. "Waffles? Cheerios? Eggs?"

"Thank you, but I'm going to grab something in town when I get to work. I have an early meeting, so I need to get going right now." Caleb leans over and kisses me gently. "Love you. Are you okay? I wish I could stay home with you today. Chin up." He puts his finger under my chin and lifts it up. He smiles that dazzling smile and kisses me one more time. Why the hell am I still texting with Sean at all? I have a great marriage now that's only gotten stronger from all the adversity. I don't need Sean anymore.

After Caleb leaves, I text Sean. *I need to clear my head. I'll let you know later.*

Going to the mountain? I'll meet you there. It's perfect. No one will hear us. By our favorite brook?

No.

That *is* where I'm going, and it's unnerving that Sean still knows me so well, that he knows exactly where I go when I need to think. I'd like to think that all the time and space that has stretched out since we were a possibility, and not just a memory, has snapped most of those threads that connected us, that let us finish each other's sentences and know what the other was thinking. Caleb should be the only one who can read me so well.

Riding the back-country roads always calms me down, especially now as everything starts waking up. Tender green shoots populate the sides of the road, and only the forsythias are in full, sunshiny bloom. Buds are on the trees and the long winter is just about behind us. Spring is the season of possibility and hope, and yet it's the time I'm most vulnerable to my demons. I've bashed them down successfully every year since I left Serenity Cove, but I don't know if I have the strength to do it again this year. The thought of whatever Sean has possibly putting Vin behind bars once and for all is a bit intoxicating. But I feel like that will never happen, no matter what I do, so why even bother trying? Why put myself through that?

I turn on the radio at the next stop sign, and the song sears right from the speakers into my soul. The words feel like a sign to me:

Don't give up
Don't give up
I feel you breaking
Don't give up
Don't give up
We all need saving
Just one more breath
Just one more night; we'll all be waiting here
Don't give up
Don't give up

It's by a singer I've heard on this Sirius station before whom I like—Ryan Star—but I've never heard this one. I make a mental note to look for the song to download. I have a feeling I'll be needing it again. I pull into a spot at the ski lodge as I listen to him sing about how he's going to hold his love while she cries. As fractured as Sean and I have become, he was the one who held me when I cried at my lowest moment. He is the only one who knows the true despair and agony that Vin unleashed on me, because he was there in the aftermath. And I wonder if I should give him a chance to just talk to me. I wonder if I shouldn't give up on getting justice served, just because Vin beat me to sharing my truth.

I pull out my phone as I'm walking down the trail. It's so quiet at this time of year—after ski season and before the summer vacation rush. I take a deep breath and call Sean. I'm startled for a moment when I hear a phone ringing just ahead of me around the bend. I thought I was alone. It stops when Sean answers. I hang up as I turn the corner and see him.

He pulls me into a bear hug. "I knew you'd change your mind, because as much as you talk about forgiveness, which is great under any other circumstance, I know you want to watch Vin fry as much as I do."

I'm equal parts relieved that the decision was taken out of my hands to see what he has to say and creeped out that Sean just showed up when I said I wanted to be alone, but I hug him back and don't pull away when he doesn't let go. We stay like that for a moment, and I think about how Caleb would feel if someone somehow snapped a photo of us like this. He'd be devastated, even if I explained that it was nothing more than a hug. I pull away and start walking briskly down the trail.

Sean rushes to catch up. "Hey, where are you going?" he calls after me.

"I told you I had to clear my head, so that's what I'm doing. Just standing around isn't going to do anything for me."

"Well, it felt so nice to hug you again. It seems like it's been years."

"It *has* been years. It's just…" I pause, searching for the right words. "Things have been a little strained between us the last three years at least. You know with all the…" I don't want to invoke our political fracture right now. It will only lead to a fight and probably make me doubt anything he tells me about Vin. And it's not like I saw Sean a lot before this, even living in the same small town. We'd run into each other in the coffee shop or the supermarket, but never made actual plans.

Sean nods sadly. "I know. I hate how much we've grown apart because of politics. It's not really my fault. After all, I'm a cop. It's just reflexive that we supported someone who came along and said, 'You do your jobs. We have your back.' It was a little intoxicating after so many years of being vilified. I don't agree with a lot of his policies."

"You mean it felt good when someone basically said you could rough up whomever you please? Remember when he said not to put your hand over the guy's head when putting him in a squad car? You know…that kind of stuff." I shake my head. "I bet the majority of cops don't feel that way. They want to serve and protect, not follow a lawless asshole."

"Look, let's not fight again over this."

"You brought him up. I wasn't going to mention Trump. But now that you have…how do I know this isn't just a pro-Trump takedown of Vin? Of course, I don't want him to be the candidate, but he apologized to me, and by admitting what he did, there's really nothing I can say that will affect anyone's view of him at this point." I sigh—it's hopeless. "The fact that he's an admitted sexual assaulter and apologized for it will be trending on Twitter any minute if it isn't already. I haven't checked."

Sean's eyes flash with anger. "I did. He's right at the top. It said, *Candidate Vin Merdone apologizes for mistreatment of women in college before any accusations even become public*. It went on to say that he personally apologized to an anonymous woman who accused him on Facebook years ago and that he claims drugs were behind his atrocious behavior, but he's been sober for years now. It also mentioned his donation to RAINN."

"He *is* a brilliant bastard. Well, at least RAINN benefits. I know it's an amazing organization."

"Yeah, I agree—that's the one positive. But how do you feel about everything else? Doesn't all this make you angry?

"Well, of course. But I can think that he did something good and still hate him for what he did to me. I can forgive him, but not forget. There's a lot of gray here."

"I know. But he's still a horrible person, even if he comes across as a sympathetic figure."

"I bet it mentions that being a former addict is why he's running on a platform to fix opioid addiction."

"Yup. You know, I'd like to think that most women, especially progressives and staunch 'Me Too' supporters will see through his bullshit, but Alyssa Milano already tweeted that she's impressed with his ability to take ownership of his actions." Sean chuckles and shakes his head. "She said while she's still hoping Biden runs soon, since she loves his work with the 'It's on Us' campaign, she thinks Vin would be a great cabinet member or even VP."

"What? Alyssa freakin' Milano likes him? This world is going to hell in a hand basket."

"I love when you use those cute, totally archaic phrases." Sean smiles disarmingly, and suddenly I'm nervous that I'm alone in the woods with him. I was sure that all of my feelings for him were long gone, but for just a second that warmth—that electric connection—zipped through me. And it feels far too dangerous, even though I would never cheat on Caleb. At least that's what I want to believe about myself. Five years ago, I may have considered it for a moment, and I may have even felt justified. But now I'd have zero justification.

"Let's walk," I say staring straight ahead as I take off. I'm a fast walker. Never been a runner, but I always walk with determination, swinging my arms, propelling myself ever forward. When my boys were little, I'd pull them along with me. At a theme park, a street fair, even the mall, I'd barrel my way through the thickest crowds, clutching a tiny hand in each of mine. I wouldn't push people, nor would I be rude. I'd just move ahead and keep moving, even though I was usually smaller than everyone around me. Now the boys gently tease me for my determined gait—it always propels me several steps ahead of them, even though they tower over me.

I'm leaving Sean in the dust, too. And when he finally catches up with me, he bends over, huffing and puffing. "Why'd you run away like that?"

"Look, I didn't ask you to meet me here. You just showed up uninvited. I said I needed to clear my head, and this is how I clear my head…walking fast through the woods."

"Okay, fine. Can we sit here? I know this was always your favorite spot." Sean sweeps his arm in front of us.

It's a beautiful vista, to be sure…a babbling brook, trees still mostly bare, but with buds ready to burst forth into an explosion of green. Sean motions behind us to a fallen log. We sit. I pull a protein bar out of my pocket and take a swig of water before I tear it open.

Sean nods approvingly. "I'm so glad to see that through all of this, you're eating."

"Ever since I got back from Serenity Cove, I keep protein bars with me all the time so I never faint again. I don't want to ever go back to that." I stare straight ahead at the water gently flowing over the smooth rocks glinting in the sunshine. Soon, definitely by early May, this whole area will be under a blanket of shade, but right now the sun feels good on my face. And each bite of my bar feels like a small victory. Every time I eat when I'm not that hungry I know I'm further away from a relapse.

"Okay," Sean begins. "Do you want to know what I've found?"

"What?"

"Well, it implicates him in Gina's murder."

"Get the fuck out of here. Are you serious?"

Another voice from behind me, "What the fuck is going on?"

I whip my head around to see Caleb standing behind me. "Caleb! Hi! You remember Sean." I gesture to him.

"Yeah, of course I remember your ex-boyfriend whom I didn't think you saw anymore."

Caleb's perfect grammar breaks my heart a little right now, because even when he's mad—he's still proper. Sean snickers quietly so only I can hear it. "He was never my boyfriend—you know that—and he followed me here. I didn't ask him to come here. He wanted to talk to me about evidence he's found on Vin. I told him I needed to clear my head, and he knows that this is my favorite spot to do that."

"So, do I—that's why when I came home for lunch and saw you weren't there, I checked your location and decided to meet you here with a picnic." Caleb holds up a basket that normally sits gathering dust on the top of our refrigerator. "I figured since you came here, you must still be stressed, so I wanted to cheer you up. Plus, you know I hate when you walk in the woods alone. I don't understand how it doesn't make you nervous."

"I used to tell her the same thing," Sean says, prompting a glare from Caleb.

"And I find you here with him." The last word is dripping with disgust so palpable I can almost taste it.

"Caleb, it's nothing. I swear. There is absolutely nothing going on between us. I told you, he just showed up here because I kept brushing off his texts about Vin. I told him it's over with Vin—there's nothing I can say that will affect Vin or the way voters feel about him since he already admitted everything. I only have to hope that it leaves a bad enough taste in people's mouths that he won't go far."

"And did you tell him that we agreed last night that it's better for you to just continue the path you're on? We can't lose you again if you go down the rabbit hole of searching for other stuff Vin has done?"

Sean stands up and looks down at Caleb. He's got a few inches on him, even though Caleb is tall himself. "Why don't you let Kate make her own decision with this?"

Caleb stands up straighter and is almost eye to eye with Sean. "She can make her own decisions, but she also has a family to think about. Our boys lost their mother for weeks, even months when she was chasing theories about Vin five years ago. She stopped eating. She fainted when she picked our boys up for school. You didn't live through it. You weren't there for her, so you should just sit down and shut the fuck up."

For a second, I'm terrified that Caleb and Sean will fight each other. I'm ready to get in between them, but they each retreat. Sean sits back down on one side of me on the log, and Caleb quickly lowers himself on the other side. "Fucking Trump supporter," I hear Caleb say under his breath. I glance at Sean. If he heard him, he doesn't show it.

"Okay," I say as brightly as I can muster. "Why don't we all just take in the beauty of this spot for a minute and just breathe." I have rarely seen Caleb this agitated.

"I wasn't there for her because you told me not to be there. You told me not to text her when she was in that program. Don't forget that."

"How does your wife feel about Kate?" Caleb asks pointedly. "Does she know you still have feelings for her?"

"What the hell? I do not have feelings for Kate. This is about bringing down Vin."

"So, your wife knows you're here right now?"

"Nicole knows I'm working. This is part of my work. Vin is a criminal, and it's my job to bring him down."

"He's also a threat to Trump, but you already knew that. Why do you need Kate to help you bring Vin down? He already admitted what he did to her. He already apologized. Believe me, I'd like to rip the guy limb from limb for what he did to my wife, but I don't want her involved in your takedown. It's too risky…to her psyche, to her health, to her recovery. If you have such damning evidence on Vin, why don't you just take him down yourself?"

"Why? Well, let's see who would you believe more…a liberal woman or a male Trump supporter? People will just think I'm doing a hack job on him."

"Is this about Kate or protecting Trump? Because throwing her into this to be possibly vilified and for Vin to know who she is, to see her face, isn't right. Oh, and it's whom would you believe, not who. Learn proper grammar." Caleb glares over me at Sean.

"You really are a stick up the ass, aren't you? You must be a joy at parties." Sean snickers.

"Enough!" I yell. "I'm hiking back to my car now. You two can work this out on your own."

"But Kate, I didn't tell you the evidence I found."

Caleb says, "Let her go."

But Sean continues. "I'm going to Vin's rally tomorrow night. I hope you'll meet me there. We can confront him together."

I spin around. "Are you out of your fucking mind? I don't want to be in the same place Vin is ever again. I don't want to look at him. I don't want him to see my face. I don't want to confront him." I breathe out heavily and blink back hot tears threatening to spill over. "He asked for my forgiveness yesterday. But I forgave him a long time ago—it was the only way for me to survive. It's still the only way for me to survive. Understand?"

I turn and walk away, but something Sean says stops me in my tracks.

"What about Gina? What about justice for Gina? It wasn't Albert Jones. It was Vin who murdered her. I'm sure of that."

I slowly turn around. "What makes you say that? How can you be so sure?"

"Forensic genealogy. It's a pretty new field, but lots of cold cases have been solved in just the past year using it. There was still some DNA preserved from under Gina's fingernails." Sean pauses and looks pained. "She clawed at and scratched her assailant, trying to defend herself. DNA testing was so rudimentary back then that it didn't yield much in terms of evidence, and it never matched anyone already in the database. And then Albert Jones confessed, so there was no need to pursue anyone else."

"And like I told you, I saw on those boards. A lot of people didn't think Albert did it," I add.

"Right. That was what got me thinking that maybe I should look into it a little, even though those boards are usually full of kooks. I did it because you begged me to."

Caleb looks pained. Maybe he remembers making me feel like an idiot when I first brought up my theory that maybe Albert Jones wasn't Gina's killer. He's probably more upset about the fact that Sean believed me and did something about it. But Caleb is a different person now than he was five years ago. I think my being away made him realize how much he needs me, and the fact that I could have starved myself to death made him appreciate me. He's not condescending anymore. What we went through made us both appreciate what we have. And the world is different now. Things just feel...heavier, and it often feels like everything outside of us is crumbling, so we cling to each other as society gets uglier and uglier. And that's what made me grow further apart from Sean. That he could still accept and support that ugliness, well it fractured us.

But five years ago, Sean listened to me when Caleb didn't. So, I feel like I owe it to him to listen to what he has to say now. As hard as that is and as much as it may upset Caleb. I turn to Caleb. "Honey, I need to hear this. Gina was my friend. If there's a chance that true justice can be served, I need to just...I need to just listen."

Caleb sighs loudly. "Fine. Listen to what he says, but I don't want you getting involved. I don't want you anywhere near Vin."

Sean interjects, "She's a big girl. Maybe stop trying to control her so much. Not a good look for you."

"Sean!" My words are steel, "Don't talk to Caleb like that. He's only looking out for what's best for me. He's worried about me."

"Well, believe it or not, I want what's best for you, too. And I think getting closure with Vin and getting justice for Gina is what's best. Now, do you…"

"Listen, Asswipe, you don't know what's best for my wife. Do you understand? If she wants to talk to you about this fine…but if you put her in any danger, you will regret it." Caleb bites each word off and spits them in Sean's face.

"Just tell me what you found," I snap. "I appreciate both of you fighting for what you think is best for me, but it's enough. This isn't a fucking schoolyard."

Caleb's face reddens as he turns away, and I feel momentarily horrible for snapping, but I don't have the patience to deal with their alpha male posturing right now. If there's evidence that points to Vin, I want to know.

"A while ago I sent the DNA to a company that does composite sketches based on cold case DNA and then ages the sketch to today. I just got back the results, and the person looks a lot like Vin. Dark hair, brown eyes, silver at the temples. That's now. Back then, the killer would have been a lot younger than Albert Jones. And get this, Albert Jones had blue eyes. He couldn't have done it."

"Hate to say it, Sean, but that's not a slam dunk. I thought you were going to tell me that it was a direct DNA match. You know, Vin admitted that he had been arrested. Wouldn't his DNA be in the system?"

"Only his fingerprints are. There was no need to collect DNA for the drug cases, and the assault was also open and shut. He got arrested at the scene. Now that I know the DNA matches his physical appearance, I just need to get a sample." Sean pauses and sighs loudly. "Look, I've risked my career to pursue this. My chief doesn't know that I took the sample. It was buried, literally, in the forensics lab."

"How did you even know to look for it?" I ask, a bit skeptical that he even has the right crime. Maybe he grabbed the DNA from some other murder by a brown-eyed man.

"I knew that murder case DNA is preserved for several decades, or at least it should be, so I started digging around. Remember, I told you about the person who placed him at the mall and recanted? I bet Vin *was* there, and she recanted because he threatened her." Sean glances at Caleb, looking like the cat who ate the canary. "So, like I said, now I just need to get a DNA sample."

"And how do you plan on doing that?"

"Well, here's the interesting thing...you don't need a search warrant to get DNA off of something that's been discarded. I'm going to go to the rally tomorrow and watch to see if he throws out a coffee cup or a piece of gum. Ever notice how he's always chewing gum? I'm guessing he'll throw it out before he speaks. I volunteered for security detail. So, I'll be right by the stage."

I'm a bit horrified. "First, ew...that's disgusting, fishing his chewed gum out of the garbage. Secondly, don't you need to wear gloves or you'll compromise the sample? Even I know that just from watching cop shows."

"I'll wear gloves." Sean seems a bit defensive. I glance at Caleb. He's tapping his foot impatiently.

"How are you going to root through the garbage wearing gloves without anyone noticing you?"

"Look, I'll figure something out. Are you with me?"

I glance at Caleb. He shakes his head, his eyes pleading. I turn back to Sean. "No, I'm sorry, Sean. I wish you all the luck in the world, and I hope you find some solid evidence. If you do, I'll support you and add my story as corroboration. But for now, I have to just detach myself from this whole thing." I pause for a moment and shake my head. "For my sanity. I hope you understand."

Sean leans in to hug me but looks over at Caleb glaring at him and backs away. "Good to see you, Kate. I understand. I hope you'll change your mind, though."

Caleb reaches for my hand, and we turn to walk away. I look back over my shoulder—Sean is watching us despondently. I have to say something. "Good to see you too, Sean. Good luck."

I want to help Sean. I really do, but I need to put my self-preservation, not to mention my husband, first. I do feel like I owe him, though—he did research for me when I needed it. And it feels impossibly sad that we've grown so far apart. It's not like the last time our friendship shattered—there wasn't one big fight this time to forgive and forget. We've just lost the connection we always had. Our differences are too vast. And still...I can't help but wonder if he would be doing this if Vin was not a threat to Donald Trump.

Caleb walks me back to my car and opens the door for me a second after I unlock it. He's nothing, if not chivalrous. "Before you go, do you want to sit at one of those picnic tables and eat?" He nods his head towards the left of us where there's a smattering of splintery picnic tables dressed in decades of lovers' carved initials and names.

Even though we weren't dating, Sean carved our names in one of the tables when we were twenty-one. We had just come back from a hike and sat down to catch our breath and eat the snacks I had packed for us. He pulled out the Swiss Army knife he always kept in a pocket and carefully carved our names. "Now we'll live on forever, at least here."

After Sean and Nicole got engaged, and I stormed out of his life, I would sometimes just sit at that table after a hike, my fingertips lightly tracing over our names, mourning what we could have been. I was so stupid. "I'm not that hungry, because I had a protein bar just now," I tell Caleb as I slide into my car. "I'm sorry. It was so sweet of you to pack a picnic. If you didn't eat yet, I can sit with you."

"That's fine," Caleb answers, though he seems disappointed. "I'll just eat at my desk."

"Okay. Love you."

Caleb sighs and turns towards his car as he answers, "Love you, too."

I turn the car on but turn it off after a moment and jump out. I rush over to Caleb's car as he's about to pull out. I wave at him to stop. He rolls down the window and asks, "What's wrong? Are you okay?"

"Yeah, I'm fine. But we should sit and have lunch. We never get to do that. And you're right, I should have more than a kid's protein bar for lunch." Caleb's face lights up as he puts the car in park and turns it off. When he steps out, he wraps me in a hug and kisses the top of my head.

"I think it's good for you to just sit here for a bit, and definitely good for you to eat more. You're having a tough time, but you can't starve yourself or even cut down. I can't lose you again."

"I know—that's what made me decide to stop you. I kind of wanted to just wallow in my feelings and be by myself, and I'm definitely not hungry, but that wouldn't have helped me." I pause and look around. "Fresh air and sunshine and food...and you," I go up on my tiptoes and kiss Caleb, "will help me."

Caleb pulls out the picnic basket and places it on one of the benches. He takes out the tablecloth that came with the basket and drapes it over the table. I breathe a sigh of relief, because he chose the table where mine and Sean's names are engraved, and I'm glad he won't see them. Of course, he probably wouldn't notice them in the tangle of decades of lovers, but even the slim chance he would is too much for me. I would have suggested we change tables for some made up reason—better view, more or less shade, anything.

Caleb hands me a peanut butter and strawberry jam sandwich, my usual lunch. I know...it's a child's lunch, but I love it for the comfort and simplicity. As I take my first bite, Sean walks by. He seems deep in thought, so I don't yell out to him. But he looks up and notices us anyway. He waves and smiles. Still, I can see the worry creasing his brow. *Not my problem*, I tell myself.

Caleb is watching me watching Sean, so I simply say, "Have a good afternoon, Sean," and turn back to Caleb. I put my hand over his.

"Thank you for doing this, Caleb. It was unexpected and just what I needed." I take a swig of water before another bite. "And I'm eating a sandwich right after eating a bar. I don't think I've ever done that. I usually let whatever I've eaten 'digest,' as dumb as that sounds."

"It doesn't sound dumb, and I'm proud of you. Just keep eating one meal at a time, and this whole Vin thing will blow over before any damage can be done to your recovery."

It's amazing to me that I'm still considered 'in recovery' after five years, but the fact of the matter is that I will always be in recovery. You're never really cured…an eating disorder can rise up and bring you to your knees at any time. And every bite I take, even if it's just a peanut butter and jelly sandwich takes me one step further away from that.

"Let's have a pizza party tonight, like we used to when the kids were little," I suggest in between bites. "It's family night, so no sports practices and no homework. The district started doing it twice a year, so the kids get a break."

"That sounds fun. Do you think we can get them to not head off into their caves for the night?"

"Maybe if we play a board game and offer an iTunes card as the prize," I laugh, but I'm half-serious.

It turns out that the boys are happy to have pizza and play Monopoly with us, though when I pull out my phone and suggest a family selfie, I'm met with groans and threats of retreating to their rooms, so I acquiesce. I'll just have to remember the moment in my head, which is probably more special, because I'm actually *in* the moment, not trying to get the perfect shot.

"We should do this more often," I say wistfully. "Remember when you guys were little, we'd have pizza and play a board game every Sunday night?"

Jacob smiles, "Yeah. I remember...especially since I'd kick all your butts every week."

"Hey, not true," Oliver protests. "I'd win plenty of times."

"Yeah, right."

"Okay...I remember both of you winning, so let's leave it at that."

"Whatever," Oliver rolls his eyes. He's right in that spot of fifteen-year-old angst. Jacob went through it and is a little mellower now...but it still often feels like he doesn't have much use for us. Someone told me they come back around at twenty-five. That's when they realize their parents aren't out to make their lives difficult and that everything we do is out of love.

"So," I say brightly, looking to change the subject, "Tell me something interesting that happened at school today."

"Nothing interesting ever happens at school," Oliver answers with another eye roll.

"Maybe not for freshman, but juniors..." Jacob counters.

"Juniors what?" I ask; he's piqued my curiosity.

"Well, we get to take classes that have real world stuff, not stuff you'll never use. Like instead of global, and learning about stuff that happened forever ago, my American social issues class talks about stuff going on now."

"Yes! I loved meeting your teacher for that class—Mr. Dunn, right?" Jacob nods. "I remember he was so engaging at back to school night, and we had a good talk at parent-teacher conference. He admitted that he hates Trump too—I think we talked about that more than you, since you're such a good student." I give Jacob a little hug, since I'm next to him on the couch, and he doesn't even pull away. "He said he never talks politics with parents, but my phone lit up with an alert from an anti-Trump Twitter account while we were talking, and he saw it and laughed. He apologized for being 'unprofessional.' I told him it made me like him more."

"Yeah, he's awesome. He's going to meet a bunch of us at the rally for that new guy tomorrow night. What's his name? Vin something, right? Mr. Dunn said that it's a great lesson for us to go to a political rally, and to have a presidential candidate here is a pretty big deal."

"I don't think you should go," I say quickly, as Caleb glances up at me, concern invading his features.

"Why not? What could you possibly find wrong with this?" Jacob asks, clearly annoyed. "Look, I know you're over-protective, but really, *Mother*... I thought you'd be excited. You always tell me I should be 'engaged' politically." Jacob uses air quotes around engaged. He's right, I tell him that all the time. I'm silent, panicking, trying to think of some plausible reason for him not to go.

"That's what I thought—you don't have a reason."

Caleb pipes up, "Maybe she's worried about possible gun violence."

"At a Dem rally? They're all about climate change and legalizing marijuana everywhere. Maybe if you're worried about all the pot smoke now that the new weed store opened in town, I could see that..."

"Dad's right. Gun violence. What if some renegade gun rights person shows up with an AR-15 strapped over his shoulder saying no one will take his guns away without a fight?" I love my brilliant husband.

"That's ridiculous. They'll have tons of security, and they're not even letting people in with bags. Mr. Dunn told us not to bring a backpack because we won't get in.

"You know, I'll be able to vote in the next presidential election. I'm sure you don't want me voting for Trump, so shouldn't I get to see a Dem candidate who may get to face him?"

"He'll be out of the race before it even gets going," Caleb says. "He's a nobody."

"Mr. Dunn told us that he's a millionaire who invented an app to help people overcome drug addiction. Plus, he rides a motorcycle and doesn't dress like someone's dad."

"Hey...someone's dad right here," Caleb protests, waving his hand. He's probably trying to change the conversation, and I love him for it.

"He went to Rolling Green. Did you know him, Mom? That would be wicked cool."

I take a deep breath before answering. I could lie and just let it go. I can't control whom my son supports politically. I always taught him to be an independent thinker. I could just say, "Yes," and not elaborate. I could tell him I knew him, and he's a horrible person, but then he'll want details...and I don't know if I'm ready to share them yet. Someday when he's a little older, I may tell him—perhaps as a cautionary tale that if you hear someone screaming in a dorm room, call for help.

"The name sounds familiar. I think we had friends in common. I may have met him once or twice."

"Cool."

I could leave it at that. But I can't. "You know, I heard he wasn't very nice in college. And he even admitted on TV that he treated girls very poorly."

"Yeah, I know. We talked about it in social issues. Mr. Dunn asked if we thought people can change and whether they deserve a second chance. He also asked if bad people can do good things and good people can do bad things."

"Wow, that's very interesting." I desperately want to dig deeper and see what Jacob thinks about Vin's behavior in particular, but I know I'll say too much. And I may start crying.

"Yeah. He said that there aren't too many people who are good or bad, but lots who are both. He called it a 'gray area.'"

"So, do you think that someone who is a bad person, who's done lots of bad things can do good things, too?" I ask.

"I do," Oliver jumps into the conversation, surprising me. "I mean, do you think all Republicans are bad and all Democrats are good?"

"I, um…I don't think that. No."

"It seems like you do…both of you."

I never thought that Oliver even paid attention to mine and Caleb's political conversations. He's usually absorbed in his phone, even if he's in the same room. "No, no…neither of us think that. There are good Republicans, lots of them…especially the ones who stand up to Trump. And there are bad Democrats. Not as many, but some have done bad stuff. And I believe Vin Merdone may be one of them."

Oliver shrugs. "Okay. I was just wondering…"

"Thank you for asking, Oliver! I love talking with you guys like this. Right, Caleb?" Caleb nods. "You've both grown into such thoughtful, intelligent young men. Let's keep having conversations like this, okay?"

"Ugh, Mom, don't get so excited." And Oliver's fifteen-year-old self is shining through again.

"Okay, Oliver."

"Can we finish the game up? My friends are waiting for me to get on Xbox," Oliver says impatiently.

"Your friends can wait."

"So, I'm going to tell Mr. Dunn I'm going tomorrow night to the rally," Jacob says as he moves his dog game piece around the board and lands on Atlantic Avenue.

"Hey, you owe me rent," Oliver says.

I just sit back and take in the moment. If there's one thing I've learned, it's that small pockets of peace when your mind is full of turmoil need to be relished. I put Vin out of my mind for now. I can't stop Jacob from going to his rally, but I sure as hell can make sure that I don't give in to Sean and go confront Vin in front of my son.

As I get into bed a few hours later, I ask Caleb, "Do you think I should have told Jacob not to go tomorrow night?"

"You can't stop him, hun. And he's right—he should be more politically engaged with the way things are. He'll be voting. And yeah, there's the whole 'Blue no matter who,' thing, but it's good for him to know about all the candidates. Even Vin."

"I know you're right," I agree as I rub moisturizer on my face. I roll on the sleep-inducing essential oil I always have on my night table. I need a good night's sleep. "Good night. Love you."

"Love you, too." Caleb answers as he leans in for a kiss.

"Sorry I'm too tired and stressed for any, um, fun. You okay?"

"I didn't expect anything. You've had a day alright. I just wanted to kiss you. Go to sleep."

"Thanks," is all I get out, before my eyes close.

I shoot up with a gasp and grab my phone off my night table to check the time…3:12 a.m. I have a lot of nightmares, but this one was one of the worst. Gina stalked me up and down winding dirt roads that climbed into darkness and then suddenly plunged down, sending me crashing through trees and thick underbrush trying to get away from her. A knife was plunged into her heart, blood blooming bright red across her hot pink parka. She was wearing that parka the night she was killed. That's part of why it was so surprising that no one noticed her body for two days, upside down in her car. Her coat came down to her knees; you'd think the hot pink would have caught someone's eye.

I remember that coat vividly. I told her how much I loved it the week before she was killed. It was the first time she wore it, and it perfectly captured her strong, yet feminine and ebullient personality. The thought of that beautiful pink coat stained with her blood haunted me for months, the fluffy softness no match for a sharp dagger. I dreamt of her in it many nights, but this is the first time she's shown up in my dream wearing it in years. And it's the first time she's been menacing—pursuing me relentlessly. I don't need a psychology degree to analyze this dream—I'm wracked with guilt over not joining Sean in trying to get to the bottom of whether Vin murdered Gina.

I want to respect Caleb's request that I not get tangled up with Sean in this. And I definitely don't want Jacob finding out what Vin did to me, so confronting Vin at the rally is out. But I also don't know if I can turn my back on Gina—after all these years, she deserves justice if Albert Jones was not the murderer…and Vin was.

I try to decide if I should just get up now and start my day, since I know with this conundrum swirling around my head, I'll never get any rest. But I roll some more essential oil onto my wrists and temples and breathe deeply. I can't function on three hours of sleep. I turn over and watch Caleb sleeping peacefully, his eyelashes lush fringes dusting his cheeks. Those eyelashes are wasted on a man, but they're one of the reasons I fell for Caleb.

Gazing at him, I know I can't do anything to fracture the fragile peace that we made with each other five years ago. And no matter how far away we get from our darkest times, I know it's still fragile. Just like with the recovery from an eating disorder, we have to work to not fall back into misunderstandings, anger and walls rising up between us.

My alarm jolts me awake at 6:30, so I must have fallen into a fitful sleep at some point. Last time I checked my phone, it was 4:02. I haul myself out of bed as my phone chimes with a text. It's Sean again. Maybe he doesn't sleep either. I wonder how Nicole feels about him texting me in the wee hours of the morning…maybe the minute he opens his eyes.

Are you sure you don't want to go to the rally? We can end this together, tonight. I'll be there to support you.

I have no idea why Sean thinks my going to the rally can end Vin's presidential run, so I don't bother answering him. If he thinks I'm going to fish Vin's gum out of the trash while he keeps a lookout, he's wrong. If he thinks I'm going to confront Vin, he's crazy.

I don't answer him until a few hours later, after the boys are at school, Caleb is at work, and I've done two loads of laundry. *What makes you think we can end it?*

Sean answers right away. *If you go up on stage and put a face to Jane Doe and get coverage, I think it will be over. That will distract so I can get a DNA sample.*

I'm shaking as I type out my reply. *Are you out of your fucking mind? Why would you even think that I would do any of that? I ALREADY TOLD YOU, I DON'T WANT TO BE FACE TO FACE WITH VIN! Get that through your head! Plus, Jacob is going to the rally with his teacher. He CAN'T see me confront Vin!!!*

I hit send before I can change my mind. I don't want to be mean to Sean, but sometimes he makes it so easy.

Turn on the tv. I think you need to see what's on Good Morning, Springfield.

I lower myself onto the couch. I feel dizzy as I pick up the remote, hand shaking. Brooke, Steve and Vin fill the screen again. Brooke is talking excitedly. "That's right, Vin—we received a tip that Jane Doe still lives in this area, maybe even in Rolling Green where you'll be for your rally!"

Vin's face transforms, his dazzling smile muting the intensity with which he was staring at Brooke. "Are you serious? You found her?"

"We didn't find her yet, but knowing she lives here should make it much easier. We have our researchers working on it right now."

Vin turns to the camera, "Jane Doe, or whatever your name is, if you're watching, please be my guest tonight.

Please let me apologize properly in front of everyone in your community. I'm so sorry for whatever pain I've caused you." Vin's eyes well up with tears.

I turn the TV off and text Sean back. *How the hell did they figure it out??? Maybe it's someone else. Somehow. I was not the only one. I know that. And I'm pretty sure you can't name sexual assault victims publicly, right???*

I pace back and forth trying to calm myself. If I were a drinker, I'd down the bottle of whisky in the dusty recesses of my pantry. Caleb's boss gave it to him when he got his promotion, but neither of us are drinkers. He saved it simply to remind him of his success.

I grab my phone as soon as it chimes. *Did you take a screenshot of your comments and save it? Is it in the Cloud or Google photos? Maybe someone found it and hooked it to you.*

Since I did take a screenshot, I jump right on my laptop to see if Sean could be correct. I can't find anything that says someone can just see what you saved without hacking you. And for the life of me, I can't figure out why someone would hack me for no reason. I'm not famous. No one would know that I'm somehow connected to Vin. I never shared the screenshot anywhere. I try to remember if I ever told anyone else about Jane Doe, but I only told Sean back when I did it and Caleb recently.

I pick my phone up and hesitate for just a moment before typing, *Nope, doesn't work like that, Sean. Is there something you want to tell me? Maybe you told someone.*

I didn't tip them off. Why would I do that? And wouldn't I give them your name if I were going to do that?

Sean has plenty of reasons to out me—it would force my hand—but he's right, he would just give them my name. Maybe I'm becoming paranoid. I feel a panic attack coming on, and I grab my peppermint aromatherapy out of my purse and rub it on my temples. I breathe slowly and deeply until my stomach expands, and I practically look pregnant. It's helping a little, but not enough, so I stick my lavender neck wrap in the microwave and pull a fluffy blanket out of the linen closet.

When I'm on the couch with my neck snuggly ensconced in lavender and the blanket wrapped around me, I pick up my phone and find the song I heard in the car yesterday. *Don't give up. Don't give up. I feel you breaking...* I let the tears flow.

I wish I still had a dog to cuddle right now. We had a dog until she passed away last year. We adopted her after I came back from the Hamptons. She was a nine-year-old lab/pit/German shepherd mix, or at least that was what the shelter told us. I didn't care what she was, I fell fast and hard for her. Caleb tried to talk me into a younger dog. He was worried the boys would be heartbroken if she passed away in a year or two, but I wanted to spoil her. I wanted her to know love and not only loneliness, fear and rejection. I named her Rose. She had been through so much; it took her time to trust us. But, when she finally did, she was my Velcro dog. And she lived to be thirteen, so we had her for four amazing years. When she passed away last year I was gutted and couldn't bring myself to rescue another dog when still I felt her presence so acutely.

I would love to be able to bury my face in soft fur, breathe in and just feel that comfort and unconditional love. Hopefully, I will one day soon. I'm almost ready. Right now, though...I am breaking. I know that, but I also know that I'm stronger than all this. I've overcome so much. I know I can get to the other side. It's just...not easy. I wish that I could predict if coming forward as Jane Doe would help or hurt that journey. Silence and pushing things down, embracing forgiveness and moving on with my life was what I needed five years ago, but now... Well, I just don't know anymore. I know that Vin admitted to assaulting me, but he certainly won't face any justice unless I make clear the viciousness of his crime. And unless the victim presses charges, the perpetrator walks. Always.

I close my eyes and lean back into the lavender, the music swirling around my brain. The next thing I know, it's two hours later and my phone is incessantly buzzing. I had turned off the ringer before—I didn't feel like seeing any more of Sean's texts for a while. As I lift it; the ringing stops, having gone to voicemail. There are five missed calls, all numbers I don't recognize. I click on my voicemail and have to play the message twice. It seems like a prank.

"Hi, Kate. This is Nelson Smith from the New York Times. I'd like to talk to you about Vin Merdone. It's been said that you're Jane Doe. You would be doing a big service to our readers and those curious about Mr. Merdone as a candidate by sharing your story with us. Don't worry, as a sexual assault victim, we will keep your identity hidden, unless you wish to speak publicly..." He goes on to ask me to contact him on either Signal or WhatsApp. The next four messages are versions of the first. *The Washington Post*, *The Wall Street Journal*, *The Daily Beast* and *Vox* all want to talk to me. I rub more peppermint oil on my wrists and temple and breathe deeply, but the fact remains that all the peppermint in the world couldn't calm me down right now.

CHAPTER EIGHT

WHEN CALEB GETS home from work, I'm in the basement knee deep in detritus—old toys, outgrown clothes, long forgotten school papers. I'm not a hoarder, but I'm overly sentimental, and I have a tendency to keep *everything*. I know; that sure sounds like a hoarder, but I don't keep garbage, I keep stuff that means something, even if it's just to me. That stained, old baseball jersey that Oliver outgrew long ago—that was what he was wearing the first time he stole home to win the game. He slid into home, and even though I doused the jersey in pre-wash stain treatment, those streaks never came out. But I looked at it as a memory and folded it away at the end of the season. The jumbled brush strokes on oak tag—Jacob painted that when he was four, and I was convinced he was an art prodigy. And then there are all the toddler toys that I saved just in case we had another baby. Just in case that miscarriage at eleven weeks wasn't the end, but just another blip on our way to growing our family.

I'm forty-six years old now. If I couldn't get pregnant again in my thirties, it's not happening now. I gave up on getting pregnant again a long time ago—it's time to get rid of the remnants of that hope and move on. Oh, and cleaning out all this crap helped me forget the shit show that has descended upon me for even a little while. It certainly makes Caleb happy when he finds me.

"Hey, you're cleaning out the basement! That is so awesome. I'm proud of you. Maybe we can make it into a man-cave for the boys. They can hang out down here with their friends."

I have felt never-ending guilt that the basement of this old house isn't fit for hanging out, because it's stuffed with, well, stuff. And Caleb used to push me all the time to clean it out, which made me feel even more guilty and more overwhelmed. But now I want to be overwhelmed with something other than the reporters knocking down my virtual door. "Yup, I thought it would be a good thing to tackle to get my mind off of stuff."

"You mean Vin? Or is there something else going on?"

"Yes, Vin. But apparently, I've been outed as Jane Doe, and I've been getting calls from reporters all day. I turned my phone off."

"Holy shit. Did anyone else know besides me?"

"Just Sean."

"Of course, he knew," Caleb snickers. "Do you think…"

I cut off Caleb. "I asked him. He said it wasn't him."

"And you believe him?"

"Well, at first on *Good Morning, Springfield* they talked about it with Vin and said they didn't have a name yet, they only got tipped off that Jane Doe lived in the area. Sean asked me why he wouldn't just give my name, which is a good point."

"I don't know—maybe he knew they could find you. Maybe he gave the first tip without your name to throw you off and then tipped off a reporter or someone with your identity."

"I guess, but that seems so complicated."

"Have you heard from him? Is he still trying to get you to go to the rally?"

"I turned off my phone, remember? He was the one who told me to turn on *Good Morning, Springfield* when they were talking to Vin about finding Jane Doe."

"Don't you think that's suspicious, Kate?" Caleb is staring at me. "How would he know they would be talking about you? Do you think he would just be sitting around watching morning TV? Isn't he a detective or something?"

"Yeah, he is..."

"So, wouldn't he be at work?"

"I guess. I don't know how he'd know. Maybe I just don't want to believe he'd be such an asshole. He was my best friend for a long time. He helped me get through so much after Vin. Why would he purposely try to destroy me?"

"Vin is a threat to Trump. Maybe that's enough for him to betray you."

"Or maybe he really does think it would be good for me to come forward. Maybe he's forcing my hand because he knows I'd never have the courage to do it myself."

"You are *very* courageous." Caleb wraps his arms around me and kisses the top of my head, my instant shot of calm. "Don't forget that."

"It's just...I was thinking right before I got the calls from reporters about whether it would be easier for me to move forward and come out on the other side if I just own my truth, or if it's better if I continue to just stay silent and push it down. I don't know."

"That's something only you can decide. I can't tell you what to do. But I'll support you either way."

"I guess I should turn my phone back on. I don't even know what time it is. I've been down here for hours."

"Did you get rid of anything or are you just looking through it?"

"I did," I say as I wave my hand over to the other side of the basement where there are a few cardboard boxes lined up with donations and recycling."

"What made you decide to do this now? Not that I'm not happy about it. I'm extremely happy." Caleb looks around smiling.

"I needed to distract myself. So, I figured doing something constructive would be good, but now I feel overwhelmed that I need to finish."

"You did enough. No one comes down here anyway. Just finish it when you can. Let's go upstairs. The boys should be home any minute. Anything for dinner?"

"Ugh, I didn't even plan dinner, and Jacob wants to go to the rally. I walk over to the large metal shelf in the corner filled with kitchen staples. "Looks like it's a pasta night," I say as I pull a box of rotini and a jar of marinara sauce off the shelf."

"Sounds good to me. I need to answer some emails before dinner. I'll just be in the office."

The boys bound in, dropping their bags and gear by the door, as I drain the pasta and heat up the sauce. I feel a little guilty that we had pizza last night, and now we're having a carb laden meal again. But I just honestly could not put any thought into dinner tonight. And it's my boys' favorite meal, besides pizza, anyway.

"Wash up for dinner, please. It's ready," I tell them as they come in the kitchen.

They're back at the table in record time. I doubt that they even used soap, but I don't care.

"Remember, I have that rally tonight," Jacob says as I spoon marinara over his pasta and grate some parmesan cheese on top.

"I know. Is your teacher still meeting you there?"

"Yup, so I don't want to be late. Gotta bounce in a minute."

"How are you supposed to eat?" I ask, a bit annoyed.

"Okay, five minutes. You know what I mean. I have to leave soon, maybe not a minute."

"If I go with him, do I need to do my homework?" Oliver asks.

"Yes, you'll need to do it after. Sorry, bud."

"But some of the teachers said if you get a note that you went, you get an extra day," Oliver announces as he polishes off his pasta.

"Okay, so I guess for those classes you don't need to do it. Are you *sure* you want to go, though?"

There's not even any reasonable excuse I can give them for my not wanting them to go. I can't think of anything. I can't tell them the truth…that the thought of them in the same place as Vin makes me want to vomit.

"Yeah. It'll be kind of cool. And I don't have to do my Global homework at all if I go. So, um…that's really why I want to go."

"Okay. Have fun guys. Please don't come home too late." I kiss each of them on the head—I can only do that easily now while they're sitting—and go back to the stove to make a bowl of pasta for myself and Caleb. I yell, "Cal, dinner!" I don't know if I'll be able to eat my dinner or not, but I'm sure as hell going to try.

I see my phone sitting on the counter, and I realize that I never turned it on. I pick it up like a bomb waiting to go off in my hand. Reluctantly, I press the button on the side and wait for it to light up. It immediately starts chiming. I have three voicemail messages, and I don't even know how many texts. Most of them are from Sean. I put my phone back down and pick up my bowl. I sit down at the table a moment before Jacob and Oliver get up to leave, and Caleb walks into the kitchen as they walk out.

"Hey guys! Leaving already? How was school today? I didn't even get to see you. You're both in and out so quickly."

"Sorry. The rally starts soon, and I'm meeting my teacher so I can get credit for going," Jacob says.

"Yeah. I need to go too, so I don't have to do this sucky Global assignment," Oliver adds.

"Okay. Have fun and please be careful," Caleb says.

"Dad, why do you sound like Mom?" Jacob snickers.

"I just want you to be careful, sometimes big crowds and political stuff brings out the crazies."

"Um, Dad...it's Rolling Green, not New York City. Don't be so uptight."

"Love you," I yell as they walk out the door.

Caleb takes his bowl of pasta and sits down next to me. "You okay?" he asks, rubbing my back.

"Yeah. I'm just a bit afraid to check my phone. It completely blew up when I turned it back on. There had to be at least ten messages from Sean and a few more voicemails from numbers I don't know. I'm assuming they're reporters."

"Are you going to listen to the vms?"

"After I eat. I need to just get this meal down, okay?"

"Whatever's good for you."

We eat in silence, and I'm relieved that I get the whole thing down. A victory. I pick up my phone and read Sean's texts first.

Why aren't you answering me? I didn't do anything. But none of my texts are even showing as delivered. So, maybe your phone is just dead or something. When you read this, please answer. I think you should come to the rally tonight. You deserve to confront Vin and show everyone what he's really like.

The one before that said, *They're talking about you on another show. It's probably only a matter of time before they figure out who you are, so you may as well go to the rally.*

The rest of the messages are pretty much variations on that theme. Six or seven years ago, I would have been excited to get so many messages from Sean. He was my crutch and provided a way for me to escape my life without cheating on Caleb. I'm not proud of that, but it's the truth. And honestly, as awful as it may seem, I don't think it was any worse than Caleb escaping into porn every night. We both were trying to escape the rut we were in—we just went about it in different ways.

But everything changed after I was away. It was like Caleb was a different person. He had a renewed appreciation for me, for our marriage, and showed it. We rediscovered each other and remembered why we fell in love. After that, I didn't rely as much on Sean, even if we still messaged weekly or so. After Trump, our texts dwindled to maybe once a month, usually less. We've gone stretches of three, four, even five months during the last few years where we didn't communicate at all.

Now…I'm dreading seeing his name pop up. The pressure he's putting on me is just too much. Maybe if I knew for sure that it wasn't about Vin challenging Trump, I could just take it as his desire to see me get closure, but I just don't know.

My phone chimes again. *I don't see you here. I'll have to respect it, but you should at least watch it. It's live streaming on Vin's website I heard. Just watch, maybe you'll decide to act, or maybe you'll decide you can just go on forgiving him. I promise I'll be okay with whatever you choose. I just want you to be happy.*

I type back, *Thank you. My phone was off. My boys are there. LMK if you see them. I don't know why I'm so nervous about them being there. But I am.*

Understandable. I'll keep an eye out.

Even though Sean has not been the friend he always was lately, I still feel better that he's watching out for my boys. It gives me the strength to listen to some of the voicemails. The first one says, "Hello, Kate. This is Vin Merdone…" I don't hear the rest of the message. I put the phone down as sweat prickles my brow and the hair on my neck stands up. The room is getting speckly, and for a moment I think I may faint.

Caleb glances up from the newspaper he's reading now, and worry laces his features. "Are you okay, Kate? It looks like you saw a ghost."

I'm silent for a moment, just trying to breathe, before answering, "Vin called me. How the hell did he get my phone number? Do you think one of the reporters gave it to him?"

"You know, I just realized something. Is your information listed in an online alumni directory?"

"Yeah… I think so. I updated something from Rolling Green not that long ago. I changed our home phone number to my cell phone. Do you think he found it there? Of course, we didn't have a huge graduating class, but I'm sure he assaulted more than one of us. How would he know it's me?"

"Someone had to have tipped off *Good Morning, Springfield* or the newspapers that you still live here. From there it probably wasn't that hard—they just had to see who still lives here. It's not like that many people stay in Rolling Green after graduation. Do you know anyone else from your year?"

"Just Sean."

"Why don't you play the voicemail? Maybe it's not even about Jane Doe. Maybe it's because you're a registered Democrat, and he's calling people in the area."

"No, I doubt he's calling every Democrat. This is a pretty liberal town. If he did that, it would have to be a robo call, not addressing me directly." I sigh wearily. "Fine, I'll play it."

I grimace as I pick up the phone, like its weight is just too much for my hand. I click speaker as the message starts, "Hello, Kate. This is Vin Merdone. So, I've found out that you're the Jane Doe who commented on my post on Facebook; that comment has haunted me for years and was the impetus for the change in my life—a change for the better. I did a lot of soul-searching after. And I think I came out a better person at the end of it. It's what led me to a place where I could run for president. I am not the person I was at twenty, and I just want to say that I'm sorry. And I want to invite you to the rally tonight. If you come, please tell my campaign manager. Or just tell our old friend, Sean. He's doing security, and he'll let you through to the stage." I put the phone down and collapse onto the couch next to Caleb.

"What. The. Actual. Fuck?"

"I'm sorry to say this, Kate, but I told you that Sean was involved in this whole thing. I haven't trusted him from the beginning—even back when you first got in touch with him again on Facebook years ago."

"But why? Vin didn't say that Sean told him, just that Sean was working the rally. Maybe he just saw him right before he called, and it's a coincidence that he mentioned him. There's a chance Vin already knew that I'm Jane Doe before he even saw Sean. Why would Sean be friendly to him, though?"

"Maybe because he knows Vin didn't actually murder someone, but he's fabricating evidence so you'll be a part of his stupid scheme to oust Vin from the race…"

"I'll text him." I type quickly and hit send before I change my mind. *Sean. Vin just called me. He knows I'm Jane Doe. And he mentioned you. Come clean now, please and tell me if you're the one who outed me as Jane Doe. You and Caleb are the only ones who know it was me, and Caleb would never say anything—he didn't even have the opportunity. So, tell me what you've done and why.*

Sean doesn't answer me. While I'm waiting, I turn on the live stream. Vin is magnetic, pacing the stage, drawing cheers with his vision for the country. I scan the crowd when the camera pans it, looking for Jacob and Oliver. I don't see them. For such a small town, there is a huge crowd. I'm guessing he's drawn attendees from Worcester and Springfield to Boston and Cambridge. Even watching online, I can tell there is a palpable energy in the room.

I turn to Caleb, "You really think Sean fabricated the evidence he says he has?"

"One hundred percent," he answers adamantly.

"Okay, I'll do a little research, which I probably should have started doing when he first claimed to have evidence, but I just didn't want to go down that road. I didn't want to find anything. It's all so tenuous. If I see something that makes it seem like Sean is right, and Vin could have killed Gina..." I shake my head. I don't even know how to finish that sentence.

Caleb puts his arms around me. "It's okay, I'm here. I'm not going to let you spiral down. I just won't."

"Thank you. If it looks like he's telling the truth, I'll go confront Vin. I know I said I wouldn't, but I think maybe it will help me just move past everything. Not facing my fears, *nor Vin*, is pretty much talking the coward's way out." I open my laptop and go to Google. "First, I'll see if the type of DNA test he said he used even exists." I Google *forensic genealogy face reconstruction*, and immediately a company pops up that does exactly what Sean described. I show Caleb. "Well, there is a company that does that. It's not some made up technology."

"That doesn't mean anything," Caleb points out. "He's a detective. He'd know about that technology and could easily lie about it. Google *Albert Jones DNA*. That'll be more likely to bring up the truth."

"Good idea. If there *was* DNA evidence saved that can be tested better now, I bet they already tested it." The top result reads, *New DNA Tests Confirm Albert Jones Is Gina Garradon's Killer*. I turn to Caleb. "Oh my God, Caleb, you're right...about everything. I'm so sorry."

I read it quickly and suddenly feel lightheaded. "This article says that as DNA tests became more sophisticated, the family of Albert Jones requested to have the case reopened, hoping new tests of the preserved DNA would exonerate him. Instead, it confirmed that it was Albert Jones' DNA that was under Gina's fingernails. How did I miss this?"

"Well, you haven't done any research on this in about five years, right? Was it during that time?"

I check the date. "Yes, you're right. It was just a little over two years ago."

"Didn't they test his DNA for a match when he first killed her?" Caleb asks.

"No, apparently since he killed himself and admitted to the crime, police never even tested his DNA. I'm guessing that was just shoddy or maybe lazy police work. But, now with advances in forensic testing, the DNA can show a family match with a lot more accuracy."

"So, they matched it with his family member—after his family requested the test, because they thought it would exonerate him?"

I scan the article again to make sure I've got it right and turn back to Caleb, "Yup."

"Wow. That sucks for them."

"Yeah, but I don't feel that bad for them. Can you imagine what Gina's family must have gone through with the case being reopened?"

Caleb shakes his head sadly.

"Well, at least she can rest in peace now, and maybe her family has more of a sense of closure, too," I say. "I feel better knowing that he definitely killed her, and there's nothing I could have done to prevent what happened."

"What could you have possibly done to prevent Gina from being killed?"

"Well, if Vin was the one who killed her, I always wondered what if I had filed a regular police report, instead of an anonymous one? Then he may have been in jail, and Gina would still be alive." I pause, trying to figure out how to explain my train of thought. I know it doesn't make sense to have blamed myself, but that's something that weighed on my mind for decades anyway. "Okay...since Vin didn't kill Gina, my filing an anonymous report had nothing to do with it. I didn't let her killer go unscathed because her killer wasn't Vin. Does that make sense?"

"Ah, I see. But you did what was right for you at the time. You said you would have been dragged through the mud at a trial. I'm sure you were right."

"I know, but I still sometimes wonder if I was a coward. I still sometimes wonder if I could have stopped him from doing to others what he did to me." I sigh. "It would have definitely stopped him from running for president. After all, Trump is a sex offender, but he's not registered as one because he's gotten away with his crimes. I don't think a registered sex offender can run for the presidency, but who knows these days."

"Right. People get away with a lot that you'd think they never could. But you shouldn't blame yourself. You were a scared kid. And since you said he assaulted other women, they could have reported him, too."

"I know. I do feel better knowing that Gina's killer is burning in hell. And I wonder what else Sean lied to me about—maybe the other assaults and that Vin was at the mall." I pause. "The other assaults make sense, but I think he was lying about the mall. He said the person recanted her story. I bet there never even was a witness who placed him there. And I have a sinking feeling he was the one who tipped off the reporters that Jane Doe lives around here." I sigh, overcome with sadness. "To tell you the truth, I'm kind of devastated that Sean lied to me about so much." I'm more than kind of devastated, I *am* devastated. I don't know how Caleb would feel about that, though.

I'm supposed to not care if our friendship is over, but I do. More than anything, I'm in shock. I can't believe that he would lie to me about something that he knows has haunted me for decades. It just feels pure evil, and I don't know if I can forgive him. Have we gotten to the point where political views mean more than friendship? And I don't just mean me and Sean, I mean everyone. I can't even count how many people unfriended me on Facebook during the last election because of my support for Hillary. It breaks my heart.

I turn back to the live stream. Even on the screen, I can tell that the joy in the room is palpable, rippling through the diverse crowd. If Vin can bring people together, do I let what he did to me stop it? I don't know. It's one thing to forgive someone when they are far away, and you're doing it to survive, it's quite another to do it face to face. It's quite another to look at someone who has damaged you to your core and say, "I forgive you." I don't know if I can. But I need to find out.

"I'm going there. I think I need to confront him. I might tell him that his apology is bullshit." I pause, unable to contemplate my other option, but knowing deep down, it's better for me to at least consider it. "I might... I might accept his apology." I sigh and shake my head. "I won't know until I see him."

"Kate, I don't think that's the best idea. You still have anonymity. No one can out you without your consent—newspapers, TV. They don't name sexual assault victims. Do you want to be scrutinized and maybe even dragged through the mud...everything you tried to avoid by staying anonymous back when it happened?"

"No, but I can't sit here and let him make everyone believe he's amazing. Sean knows me too well. He knew that I wouldn't be able to keep my mouth shut once Vin reached out to me personally. He knew that I wouldn't be able to take the high road. I think you're right that he told Vin, and I think that's why. I want to prove him wrong. Or I guess I'm proving him right."

I don't know when Sean became the villain; I just know that he hurt me deeply by lying and fabricating evidence. I don't know what he planned to *do* with that fabricated evidence, besides use it to lure me to the rally to confront Vin in front of everyone. It's not like he could go public with fake evidence. The crime has been solved and the case put to rest. I'd love to know how he planned on explaining that to me.

"Sean knows you well? Did you forget that I know you *really* well, too? I know you can take the high road. Maybe you wouldn't have been able to five years ago, but you came back from the program a different person. You forgave Vin already. Please, I'm begging you…let it stay that way. I doubt Vin's campaign will even go anywhere." Caleb pauses, before continuing, "And I know he didn't murder your friend, but what if he's still a dangerous maniac?"

I gaze at Caleb and place my hand gently on his cheek. I lean down and brush my lips against his lightly, then a bit hungrier. "Thank you," I say, as I straighten up. "Thank you for seeing my better angels and believing in me."

Caleb smiles and leans back. He takes my hand and tries to pull me down next to him, but I straighten up, and he looks confused.

"And that makes this even harder…I'm not an angel. I'm not as forgiving as I hope to be, as I want to be. I can't just push this down and close my eyes. I may be able to just walk away, but I won't know that until I walk into it." I look straight into Caleb's eyes. "When I was a scared twenty-year old, I only filed an anonymous police report. I was sure that the next time Vin did something, someone braver than I would name him, and that police report would help put him behind bars." I sigh. "But that never happened. And right now, I need to give that scared girl a voice. I need to be who I wish I were back then—a badass who faces her fears head-on."

Caleb stands up slowly. "Well, I'm going with you then."

* * *

The recreation center at Rolling Green is oppressively hot. There is a stage set up at one end of the basketball court with an arch of blue and white balloons. Vin is pacing beneath them. The court is completely full with overflow spilled onto the track that circles above us, people leaning over the steel railings. Vin's voice booms out of loudspeakers, "We need to fix what has broken us...poverty, drugs, lack of opportunity. I've experienced all of those..." I tune out what he's saying as I scan the crowd for Jacob and Oliver.

"They're over there," Caleb says, as he steers me towards them.

"Oh hey. What are you doing here?" Jacob asks.

"Well, we thought we'd see what it's all about," Caleb explains. But I feel the need to warn them.

"Listen, guys...I may say some stuff tonight that surprises or upsets you. I know Vin, and he asked me to come here. If I talk to him in front of everyone, it may be upsetting, so if you want to leave now, you should."

"What are you even talking about?" Oliver asks. "Are you going on the stage or something?"

"I don't know. Maybe." My heart is hammering in my chest. I didn't think this through very well. I'm eyeing the exit when Caleb chimes in.

"Mom is incredibly brave and came here to confront Vin. He wants to apologize to her, but Mom doesn't know if she can accept his apology. And I support her. I hope you both do, too."

"Well, yeah. We always support you," Oliver says. "But I'm confused. What did Vin do?"

I don't know how to explain this to my fifteen-year-old. I don't want to at all as I blink back the tears ready to flow. "Well, remember how I said that he treated girls poorly?"

Oliver and Jacob both nod.

"Well, it was a little more than that. He was violent with me." I pause trying to figure out my next words. "He pushed me very hard. He said he was sorry, but I don't know if he really is."

"Are you Jane Doe?" Jacob asks, eyeing me warily.

"How do you know about that? Did you talk about that in social issues class, too?"

"Yeah."

I take a deep breath. They're going to find out at some point, and if I tell them myself, at least it's on my terms. It will also remove the biggest barrier to my going public. I don't want my boys to know. I don't want my parents nor my sisters to know either, I realize, but I'll worry about that later. I hadn't even thought of them through this whole ordeal. My mom and I haven't discussed the assault in decades—I don't know if she even remembers. And I don't think my sisters ever knew. For a moment I think that the easiest thing to do would be to just lie, say "Nope, I'm not Jane Doe" and walk out. But the easiest thing isn't usually the right thing. And this is no exception.

"Yes. I'm Jane Doe." Like ripping off a bandage, quick and clean, but painful.

Jacob's eyes widen and Oliver looks confused. He asks, "Wait, who's Jane Doe?"

"Mom is," Jacob answers when I'm silent, not knowing where to go from here. "She accused Vin Merdone on Facebook of doing bad stuff in college way before he ran for president."

Oliver turns to me, "Is that true?"

I nod. "It's true. He asked me to come here so he could apologize in person. I wasn't going to do it. I didn't want you guys to know anything about this whole situation."

"Didn't he say that you helped him change?" Jacob asks.

"He did, yes."

"So, it's a good thing that you posted that stuff."

"I suppose."

"Hey, Vin...over here!" The man behind me yells practically right in my ear, making me jump. "I found JANE DOE!!"

I spin around, "This is a private conversation. Please stop."

"You can't have a private conversation in a public place, sweetheart."

"Are you a Trump plant or something?" I ask.

The guy laughs, his double chin shaking. "Maybe..." He winks before yelling again, "Jane Doe is right here. I heard her say it."

The woman next to me pipes up, "Just ignore him. He's been heckling Vin Merdone the whole night. I called over security, but they said it's his First Amendment right. I don't think Vin can hear him anyway in this big crowd."

"Thank you," I say to her before turning back to the boys and Caleb. "You know what, this was a mistake. I need to get out of here." I start to walk away while watching Vin and walk right into Sean.

"Hey! You came. I thought I heard this troublemaker yelling about you."

"Sean, you piece of shit. I'm not a troublemaker. You fucking invited me."

I glare at Sean. Of course, he invited his Trump supporter buddy. Maybe he even described me to him and told him to look out for me and text him if I showed up. Maybe it's not a coincidence that he's right behind my boys.

"What the hell, Sean?" I whisper. "Did you have this guy stand by my boys in case I showed up? I know I asked you to keep an eye on them, but not like this. I need to get out of here."

"No, don't leave. You're so close to speaking your mind. You're so close to breaking the hold Vin has had on you. Just tell him what he did to you. Put a face to the accusations. Tell him you think he murdered Gina."

"I know he didn't murder Gina, Sean. Your evidence is fake. I saw an article that the DNA matched Albert Jones. I'm done. I can't believe you lied to me, and you lied to me about something so easily proven. Why?" Sean is silent, looking down at the floor.

"Honestly, Sean, it breaks my heart. I came here to see if I could forgive Vin if I see him face to face, or maybe to tell him that I can't. But I just realized that maybe I came here to see if I could forgive you, too..." I pause and blink hard, afraid I may cry. "And I don't know if I can. Was all the stuff you told me made up?"

"No, there were the other assaults—the anonymous ones and the two arrests. That was true, but the stuff about Gina's murder... I just wanted you to tell him off, so you could get closure. And I thought that would make you do it." Sean stares down at the floor for a moment, not looking at me before he continues so quietly I barely hear him. "I thought it would be good for you. I'm sorry. I shouldn't have lied."

"I bet you tipped off the reporters about me too, didn't you?"

"I didn't tell them your name. I may have shared that I know Jane Doe lives around here. They did the rest of the research. I'm sorry." He sighs. "Again, it was what I thought was best for you. Once you were out as Jane Doe, I figured you'd have no choice but to stand up to Vin."

I look up at Caleb as I'm trying to decide how to respond. He's glaring at Sean, and I wonder if I'll need to get in between them. Caleb moves to my side quickly and gets in Sean's face, sharply whispering, "Leave her the fuck alone. If she wants to confront Vin, she will. If she doesn't want to, let her walk away." I'm sure if our boys weren't next to us, he would have been a lot louder. He never curses in front of them.

"Sean, you're basically saying, 'Okay, I did the terrible thing you accuse me of, but here's why I did it, so don't blame me.' Well, I blame you. I blame *you*. I don't care if you thought it would give me closure. That's for me to decide…not *you*."

"I'm sorry. You're right. And it wasn't because I think Vin is a threat to Trump… Just look at him."

I back away and stare at Vin on stage. He's beaming, leaning down to high five people in the crowd. Then he stands up and holds his phone up high in front of him to take a selfie with the crowd. A big cheer raises up behind him and likely crashes over him, bathing him in the adulation. It's too much for me. "Oh, he's a threat to Trump alright," I say to Sean, and I know he knows this is true. I know that's at least part of why he lied to me. And one part of me wants Vin to take down Trump, and the other part of me simply cannot bear the thought of Vin being anywhere near the Oval Office. That part wins.

I storm my way to the stage, pushing through the crowd. Sean follows right behind me. I imagine that Caleb is hanging back with the boys, possibly nervous, but I hope proud. The security guard right in front of the stage stops me, his hands up. But Sean talks over my head, "Let her go. Vin wants her up there."

The security guard nods at me and gestures for me to walk by him to the stairs up to the stage. I climb up slowly. The crowd hasn't noticed me yet—they are still cheering for Vin, who hasn't noticed me yet either. I want to back off the stage. Just retreat into anonymity, because I know that will end in a moment and things will never be the same. I wonder if this will make national news, if my parents and sisters will see it before I can tell them. Beads of sweat adorn my forehead, and I wipe them off with my sleeve. I need to look calm and cool.

Suddenly, Vin turns to face me. Recognition dawns in his eyes first, then his smile. He reaches his arms out to me. I recoil. The fear must have fallen over my face like a curtain because he speaks so quietly, I barely hear, "I won't hurt you again. I promise. The man I am now is so different from the boy I was."

The words jumble in my throat, fighting to get out, but I'm silent. I breathe deeply as the crowd quiets. They sense something is about to happen. Vin breaks the silence. "This is Jane Doe, and she deserves to be heard. As many of you know, she called me out on Facebook years ago and forced me to really examine my past. Her words forced me to confront some of my darkest deeds. Things I'm not proud of." Vin pauses and looks out over the crowd. They are staring at him, rapt. "I realized that even if I was sober and had asked for forgiveness as part of my recovery, I wasn't truly healed. I wasn't whole. I was ignoring those dark parts in me. I was denying what I had done. Jane Doe changed all of that." Vin turns to me and gestures for me to join him. "May I say your name?"

I nod. "Jane Doe's name is Kate." Silence and then thunderous applause. "Yes! Show her your appreciation. It took a lot of courage to come up here. But I invited her. I wanted to face my accuser. I wanted to be the opposite of Donald Trump who throws accusations back at anyone who dares speak the truth." Vin pauses and shakes his head. "He rains down threats on those who pull back the curtain... But I will not. I will always give a voice to those who need to raise theirs.

"Raise your voice, Kate. You can tell everyone how you feel. And I will apologize to you. I'm sorry. Always, I'm sorry." Vin's eyes well up with tears. He presses his knuckles into them for just a second, before he shakes his head and laughs ruefully. "Look at me, overcome with emotion." In all the times I imagined confronting Vin, I could never have imagined this...not in my wildest dreams. I imagined him being belligerent. I imagined attacking him, making him see me. I imagined plunging a knife into his chest. I imagined so many things. But I never imagined his tears.

"You destroyed me," I say quietly. And then louder, "I was a happy, trusting girl, and you crushed my soul. That night...the night that you invited me to take a walk with you, and I stupidly said, 'Yes' fractured my life into before and after. I replayed in my head a million times that moment when you asked me to come upstairs with you to get a sweatshirt and hated myself for following you into the elevator and up to your room." I pause and glare at Vin, tears are streaming down his face, and I can't help but wonder if they are real or simply crocodile tears.

I decide it doesn't matter and continue. Even if they are real tears, even if I am hurting him to the core with my words...good, let him feel a tenth of my pain. "I replayed in my head the moment you held the door shut over my head as I tried to pull it open. I replayed the moment you said, 'Is it going to be hard or soft?' I replayed the moment you dragged me into the bathroom stall so you could 'take a piss,' and I wouldn't be able escape. Your black satin sheets rose up in my dreams, haunting me. *You* haunted me." I shake my head and sigh. I notice a camera trained on me out of the corner of my eye and debate shutting my mouth and retreating. But it's too late now. It's a torrent gushing out. The room is silent, so is Vin, except for occasional sobs.

"The next morning, I woke up with angry amethyst bruises ringing my shoulders, five on each side, where you held me down." A look of horror crosses Vin's face, mingling with his tears. "Yes, that's right, you held me down. You locked me in your room. You dragged me to the bathroom, so you could go, and I wouldn't escape." I breathe out angrily. "You assaulted me. And I don't know if I buy that it was all because you were under the influence of drugs and alcohol." I pause again, before continuing. "If you misread my signals, thinking it was consensual, you wouldn't have thought to lock me in your room, because you would have assumed I wanted to be there. You *knew* what you were doing."

"I'm sorry," Vin whispers.

I ignore him. "You know, I was drunk, but I sobered up very quickly." A gasp ripples through the room, and I realize what I've just admitted too late. I can only hope that Caleb had somehow persuaded Jacob and Oliver to leave already, but I doubt it. I hope that it can be a teachable moment—don't make the same mistakes I did.

I turn to the audience. "Yes, that's right—I admitted that I was drunk. I was in college. And I wasn't out of my mind; I was probably more buzzed than drunk. And as I've always believed, drinking *didn't* make me a victim, violence did." I turn back to Vin. "*You* were violent. Whether it was drugs, alcohol, being young…I don't care. You were violent."

"I'm sorry. I'm sorry. I'm sorry." Vin is repeating this, a mantra, maybe even a talisman for him.

"Here's the thing…while I appreciate your apologies, I forgave you a long time ago—five years ago, to be exact. I had to. My family, my sanity, my very life were all at risk if I didn't. Forgiving you is what transformed me from a victim to a survivor. And I am, and always will be, a survivor."

I turn to walk off the stage as the audience erupts in applause. Descending, I see Sean waiting for me. He pulls me into a hug, but I pull away quickly. I don't want Caleb seeing that, but more importantly, I'm still furious with Sean. He speaks loudly over the fading claps, "Great job, Kate! You really told him."

"Fuck off, Sean." I glare at him while the shock of my words hit him. He's silent, so I continue. "You know, when you lied to me on the trail, I kept thinking that something just didn't add up—Vin wasn't rich when Gina was murdered. He was a college student. And in the years that followed he was a vagrant drug abuser, so why would they hide evidence? But I pushed that out of my head because I also thought...*why would Sean lie to me?* Imagine how I felt when I saw confirmation of just that."

"Look, I knew if there wasn't a lot at stake, you would never have confronted Vin. Like I said, I wanted you to have closure. I thought you wouldn't have done it for yourself, but maybe if you thought he killed Gina, you would have. But you *did* do it for yourself. You proved me wrong. And don't you feel better now? Don't you have closure?"

"Maybe you underestimated me. All I know is that it was fucked up of you to use Gina like that."

"I'm sorry. I didn't think it was fucked up. I wanted to see you tell him off. Didn't you need this?"

"I don't know. It felt good in the moment. It was cathartic and incredible and something I had dreamed of, but it didn't happen the way I thought it would. I always figured I'd physically hurt him if I had the chance. I used to fantasize about stabbing him, but I knew I never would."

At that moment Caleb comes up next to me, and I'm glad. I don't want to be normal with Sean yet. I want to stay mad at him for a while—that's what he deserves. Caleb wraps his arms around me from behind and kisses the top of my head. He knows that makes me feel safe—his most tender and frequent gesture. "You were amazing up there. You really put him in his place and got to say everything in your heart. I'm so proud of you."

Caleb turns to Sean. "She doesn't need you anymore. She's free of Vin's hold now, and you can take your Trump-loving, murder conspiracy theory-spouting ass out of her life."

Sean bites his words off angrily, "We were having a conversation before you interrupted. Kate was just saying that my making her go up on stage was cathartic. So, you should thank me."

"That's not what I said, Sean," I reply angrily. "I said that going up was cathartic, but I don't think your pushing me into it was right. And I still don't know if this was even about me or Trump. And I'm not happy at all that you lied to me about Gina. We need to let her soul rest in peace now."

"Yeah, I can't believe you followed Kate and made her listen to your bullshit just to get her to confront Vin. You're a fucking asshole," Caleb is boiling over with rage.

I feel like I'm drowning suddenly. I'm not ready to forgive Sean yet, but I also don't want to believe that he's a terrible person. He was my best friend for so long. He was there for me for so long. And maybe he did think it was best for me to confront Vin and get it out of my system. But, if he manipulated me because he doesn't want Vin to threaten Trump, then I can't forgive him.

"I'm going to ask you one more time... Just tell me, Sean, was this all for Trump or for me?" I ask, locking eyes with him.

"Do you expect him to be honest, Kate? He's already lied to you so many times," Caleb interjects.

"I'm willing to let him answer, and I have to hope he tells the truth."

Sean starts quietly, "I've always cared about you, Kate. And after Vin, well it killed me what happened to you. I never forgave him. And I don't think he'd be a good president. So, maybe a little of it was that. But it was mostly about you. I swear."

My stomach is in knots. Our friendship will never be the same. I know that. I can't trust Sean with my heart anymore, but it's been like that for a long time—three years. People change. But, if I could forgive Vin, I should be able to forgive Sean. It'll take time, though. "Okay, Sean. Whatever. I hope that now you'll leave me alone about Vin. It's done. I've said what I needed to say."

"Sure. I'm sorry, Kate." Sean leans forward to hug me, but Caleb steps in between us. I roll my eyes and sigh. Caleb as the alpha male is getting tiresome. Everything is getting tiresome. I just want to move on from here.

"It's enough," I whisper, though I'm not sure whom I'm talking to—Caleb or Sean.

I turn to the stage. Vin is speaking again, but I missed what he said. I hear "humbled," "life-changing" and of course "I'm sorry" again and again.

"Caleb, where are the boys? Were they okay with everything I said?" I panic, not seeing them, thinking that maybe they're upset with me.

"They're fine. They're proud of you, and they're still watching. Jacob's teacher came over to us, so I think they didn't want to be rude and walk away."

"Mr. Dunn? Did he recognize me?"

"He did."

"Oh my God. I was hoping since I haven't seen him in six months, maybe he wouldn't. But I guess that was unlikely. Did he say anything?"

"He said you're a 'bad ass.'"

"He wasn't upset that maybe this could hurt Vin's chances against Trump, if he even gets the nomination?"

"Honestly, I don't think anyone is thinking about that. Did you hear the cheer that went up for you? This is a small town. And even though there are a lot of people here from other areas, everyone from Rolling Green who knows you is proud of you. I know that."

"Do you think I'm right to forgive Vin? To say that I forgive him in front of everyone?"

"I do. I think it's what's right for you. I think that forgiveness lets you move on. And like you said, it keeps you from remaining the victim. It gives you power. When you forgave Vin five years ago, I got my wife back." Caleb pauses, a far off look on his face. "When you forgave me, it gave both of us our marriage back. I thought you were going to divorce me for my, um, problem. So, how could I not be for forgiveness?"

"Kate!" I snap my head around to Vin, as he calls my name again, "Kate! Please come back on the stage."

A spotlight falls on me as I shake my head no. Cheers erupt in the room, "Kate! Kate! Kate!"

I turn back to Caleb, "What the hell is going on?"

"I don't know. I guess you should go back up there."

Reluctantly, I ascend the steps again and stand with Vin below the arch of balloons. He turns to me. "Kate, thank you. Thank you for opening my eyes even more to the damage I've done. It was painful, but necessary. I realize that I've gone through my life enjoying my cis-gendered white man privilege, even when I was homeless, not realizing the destruction I've left in my wake."

Vin's clearly saying what a liberal town like Rolling Green wants to hear, and I wonder if he trotted out the phrase "cis-gendered white male privilege," because he believes it or because he sounds "woke." The applause and whoops say that it's working. How is it possible after everything I said that people are still cheering for him?

He turns to me. "Kate, may I give you a hug?"

I back away, knowing my disgust is palpable.

"Okay," Vin says. "No hug. I respect your space. I wanted to say thank you again for opening my eyes. I know I lashed out at you when you commented on my post years ago, but I want you to know that I am not that person. I want *everyone* here to know that I'm *not* that person, and I never will be again."

"Okay. I need to go now. Um, you're welcome. Thank you for your apology." As I turn to walk away, I suddenly realize that I should not be thanking him. I don't need to be polite. "Actually, I don't know why I'm thanking you. This was the least you could do." I turn on my heel and walk off the stage.

My phone has been buzzing in my pocket non-stop. I don't even want to look at it, but I pull it out as I walk over to Caleb. Facebook notifications clog up the lock screen. Most are mentions in Rolling Green Resists, the secret anti-Trump group I'm in. There are some texts sprinkled in from my sisters and Heather. My stomach drops. Texts from them mean that my appearance here has made national news already. Or maybe it's trending on Twitter. I can't look now. Caleb pulls me to him as I stick my phone back in my pocket.

"I'm so glad you took back your thank you. He does *not* deserve a thank you from you ever."

"Thanks. I just want to go home. Are the boys still with Mr. Dunn? I want to see them before we leave."

Caleb leads me to my boys, threading through the crowd as I hang onto his hand. I have my head down, but people still thrust thumbs-up in my face or clap me on the shoulder. One woman yells to me, "You're my hero," as I walk by her. I look up and smile, but I don't feel like anyone's hero. My insides churn, and I feel like I might either faint or vomit. I wish that I hadn't eaten the bowl of pasta. I feel a sense of closure, yes— but being thrust into the public like this is a little bit sickening…or more than a little bit.

"Mom!" Jacob greets me with a hug. "I can't believe you went up there and said all that stuff."

"Did it upset you?"

"I'm upset to know that that happened to you, but I'm not upset that you did it. I'm also not voting for Vin for sure. I hope he's not the one to run against Trump. I just won't vote."

"No, you need to vote. Hopefully, he won't be the nominee."

"Hello, Mrs. Berg," Mr. Dunn thrusts his hand out to shake mine.

"Mr. Dunn, it's so nice to see you. Jacob loves your class so much. I know I told you that back at our conference, but he loves it even more now. Thanks for teaching them the important stuff."

"Well, thank you for this teachable moment. I'll be using this in our next class. We've been talking about whether good people can do bad things and bad people can do good things. This is a perfect example. Is that okay?" I nod before he continues, "Vin seems like a good person in that he stands for issues that are important, like tackling drug addiction and fighting climate change, but he did this horrendous thing. How do we handle that dichotomy? How do you handle it so graciously?"

"I don't know. I'm sorry…" I pause. "I just know that forgiveness frees you, so I forgave Vin—for me, not for him. And I can't say that I'll vote for him in the primary…because I won't."

"Understandable."

Oliver has been quiet, so I turn to him. "Are you okay, Oliver? Did anything that happened tonight upset you?"

"I'm okay. I'm sorry for *you*. That guy's a dick."

"Oliver!"

"Well, he is," Oliver maintains.

"He's not wrong," Caleb says, and we all laugh, even Mr. Dunn, which is a bit horrifying, but the warm smile on his face melts my embarrassment, so I can just be in the moment. I can't believe that I'm laughing. I want to bottle it.

"Let's go home," I say.

Jacob turns to Mr. Dunn. "Is that okay if I leave now? Will I still get credit?"

"Of course. It's almost over anyway. Go be with your family."

"Thank you, Mr. Dunn. I really appreciate it." I clasp his hand as I say this. "You're a great teacher, and more importantly, a great role model. Thank you again. I hope Oliver gets you, too, when he's a junior."

"I hope so, too." Mr. Dunn smiles warmly at us again.

"Take care," I say over my shoulder as we make our way to the door.

CHAPTER NINE

ON THE WAY home from the rally we stop to get frozen yogurt. "Hey, Mom, they have toasted marshmallow. Are you gonna get it?" Oliver asks.

"You know what? I am…with peanut butter cups on top."

"Awesome. That's what I want, but with sprinkles and gummy bears, too," Caleb says.

"You want gummy bears?" I ask laughing.

"You're never too old for gummy bears," Caleb insists. "Right boys?"

Jacob answers, "Yup." Oliver nods as he grabs a cup.

"You guys, this is so nice. I can't remember the last time we went for frozen yogurt together."

"I remember you used to not eat it when we came here, and then you went away. So, I kind of didn't want it anymore," Oliver shares.

I had no idea that Oliver equated eating frozen yogurt with my going to the residential program, but being that he was ten, and I had a panic attack when we went a few weeks before I left, I can understand it. "Oliver, I'm so sorry you felt that way. How come you never told me?"

"I didn't think it mattered. And I was kind of embarrassed. I would have gone if you asked, but we just kind of stopped going, and you were so much better. So…" Oliver is silent for a moment. "But I get it now. I know it had nothing to do with it."

"I understand why you felt that way, and I'm so sorry." I lean over and give Oliver a hug. It's easy for others to see the effects of an eating disorder when they're looking at your skeletal frame, but they can't see the invisible effects upon those you love. And that's the hardest part to get over. You can gain weight and get healthy, but there will always be scars—little weak spots—not just in the person battling, but in everyone who loves that person. And you never know when those old scars will pop up...like now.

"It's okay, Mom. I know now it doesn't matter."

"You know, you're a smart kid, Oliver."

Jacob snorts, because...well, that's what big brothers do. "Okay, okay. Let's enjoy our yogurt." And I do, I savor each bite—not so much because it's delicious, though it is, but because it goes down easily. I have no anxiety about getting sick, even after everything I've been through tonight, even after facing Vin. I feel a lightness that I haven't felt in decades.

Caleb and I collapse on the couch after the boys retreat to their rooms like they do every night. I lean my head on his shoulder. "Should we turn on the news?" he asks quietly.

"Nope, I don't want to know what anyone is saying about me. I haven't read my texts, nor have I even checked Twitter."

"I love when you use proper grammar," Caleb says as he kisses my neck. I laugh and turn my head to kiss him hungrily. My phone keeps buzzing, but I just ignore it. I need to forget Vin and the election and baring my soul in front of what seemed to be my entire town.

"Let's go upstairs," I whisper. Just as we're about to walk up the stairs, Jacob comes out of his room.

"Anything to eat?" Which means, "Can you make me something to eat?"

"Of course—I'll find something. Do you want a snack or a meal?" I relish every moment that I feel needed by my boys.

"I don't know. I guess a small meal. Were you about to go to sleep?"

"Nah, it's fine." And even though I didn't get to make it upstairs with Caleb, it *is* fine. It's more than fine. It's been a while since I've suggested we "head upstairs," and I can see from the look on Caleb's face that even though he's disappointed, he's appreciative…and relieved that I made the first move. I turn to him and mouth, "I'm sorry."

He smiles and shakes his head, mouthing back, "Don't be."

I toast a couple of chocolate chip waffles for Jacob and whip up some scrambled eggs. My kids love breakfast at night. The smell of the waffles brings Oliver out, so I make the same for him. By the time I fall into bed just before midnight, Caleb is already sleeping, but that's okay. I don't even need my aromatherapy to fall into a deep sleep. It probably helps that I haven't looked at my phone. Anyone who needs to get in touch with me in an emergency, like my parents, would call my house. And my boys are home and safe in bed. That's all that matters as my head hits the pillow, and I'm out.

My alarm jars me awake at 6:30, and I realize that I've slept soundly through the night for the first time in ages. When I hit stop on my alarm, notifications crowd my lock screen. I scroll down as I haul myself out of bed and head into Oliver's room to wake him. Apparently, my moment of forgiveness is trending on Twitter. I guess it could have been worse. I slip my phone in my pocket and gently shake Oliver's shoulder. "Come on, bud. Get up, please. You'll be late." Oliver rolls over, muttering, "Just a little longer, please."

"Five minutes." I say, as I head into Jacob's room and repeat the whole process. I let them both sleep a few extra minutes. I'll write a note if I need to—it was an emotional night last night. I microwave French toast sticks, so they can eat quickly, and make their lunches before heading back upstairs to wake them again. I'm glad to have the distraction of getting my boys out the door this morning. When they leave, I'll need to face my phone and all the fall-out from last night.

I turn the lights all the way up in both of their rooms, and yell, "Up now!" from just outside their doors, which not only does the trick in waking them, but also brings Caleb, bleary-eyed into the hallway for back-up.

"Boys, get up and out!" he booms from right behind me.

Once they rocket through their morning routines, scarf down their French toast sticks and are out the door in record time, I turn to Caleb who's in his robe eating cereal standing at the counter. "Why don't you sit down? You have plenty of time to get ready for work."

He nods and moves over the table. I sit down next to him and weigh my options. I could tackle all of the texts and notifications, or I could thank him for his help in my own special way. "Why don't you take a hot shower, and then I'll do your very favorite thing…"

He dumps out the rest of his cereal and bounds up the stairs to the bathroom. "You don't have to ask me twice" floats down the stairs behind him.

While he's in the shower my house phone rings, and I know it's either a robo-call or my mother.

I answer as brightly as I can, "Hi, Mom! How are you?"

"How am *I*? I think I should be the one asking you that. Kate, how come you never talked to me about what happened to you? I feel terrible." Her voice falters, and I feel worse.

"We did talk about it once, Mom. Remember? A long time ago you found a letter that I had mentioned it in, and you asked me about it. I said I was okay, and we moved on. I moved on a long time ago. If Vin Merdone hadn't contacted me before the rally, I would have just kept it to myself."

"I don't remember talking to you about it. I'm sorry." Now I can hear that she's full on crying, and I feel even worse.

"It's okay. I'm fine. Look—it never stopped me from getting married, having a family, living my life. I'm a survivor. I'm okay. It's probably happened to more people than you know. I mean, look at all the 'Me Too' stuff. Even celebrities have had to deal with it."

"I know. Those bastards should all be strung up…" My mom has always spoken her mind, and as she's gotten older, her language has gotten more…colorful.

"True. And everyone who's gotten caught up in it has paid a steep price, so that's good."

"But will Vin pay a price? I won't vote for him. You know I love Joe anyway and everyone's saying he's about to enter the race."

"Yes, Mom. I know you're a Biden supporter. It seems like he'll run."

"He's better than that orange asshole in the White House now. He'll bring back class."

"I agree."

"You know I had to go back on my blood pressure pills because of Trump?"

"I know. I'm so sorry about that. I told you to stop watching the news."

"I had gotten it down walking the track at the Y and eating Cheerios and oatmeal. But he makes me so mad every day."

"He makes me mad too, which is why I hesitated to say anything to Vin. I just keep thinking, what if he was the best chance to beat him? You know, Sean is a Trump supporter, and I think maybe he tipped him off to my identity."

"Sean? Sweet Sean from college is one of them? Nooo!"

You would think I told my mom that Sean was a murderer. At least I distracted her from the reason she called. I'm more comfortable with her anger than her tears. She's a "tough old broad," and doesn't cry easily, so that makes the fact that I made her cry so much worse. "Yes, but he's a cop, so that's his reasoning."

"There are plenty of cops who don't like that monster."

"Yup. Are you feeling a little better now? You know I'm just fine, right?"

"Okay—if you say so. One question, is that why you had to go to that place in the Hamptons. Was it because of what Vin Merdone did? And is that why you were so skinny right after school?"

"Probably." It wasn't easy answering that, but it does feel good to finally own my truth.

"You know, you're still too skinny. You need some meat on you."

"I weigh at least ten or maybe fifteen pounds more than I did then. And I don't think that will happen again. Getting to speak my truth on that stage to Vin...well, it feels like a weight has been lifted. I guess it was my 'Me Too' moment."

"I'm proud of you, sweets. I didn't raise you to take any shit, and I'm glad you stood up for yourself."

"Thanks, Mom. Love you."

"Love you, too. Oh, and call your sisters. Jamie and Laura both said they texted you a bunch of times, and you haven't answered them. I told them, 'Pick up the phone and call.' But I'm sure they didn't."

"Not yet, I did see that I had a lot of texts, but I haven't checked my phone, and I didn't read them yet. I will."

"Pick up the phone and call. You're sisters, you should talk, not just text. I wanted to talk to you, so I picked up the phone, and you answered. That's how it works. You never know if a text gets read." My sisters and I rarely talk on the phone, though we do text. In fact, my mom is the only person I speak on the phone to regularly.

"I promise I'll be in touch with them. Thanks for calling, Mom. Do you feel better now?" I glance up the stairs, straining to hear if the water is still running. I don't want to break my promise to Caleb.

"I do. As long as you're okay, I'm okay. And I'm proud of you for standing up for yourself. Okay…I have to go post some Joe stuff on Facebook. I know he's going to declare soon—have to make sure Merdone gets his ass handed to him in the primary."

"Sounds good, Mom," I say as I hear the water shut off and head up the stairs.

"I'll talk to you soon. Love you much, my dear."

"Love you, too. Bye."

I leave the handset on the stairs as I head to our bedroom to wait for Caleb.

***

Fortified by our frolic, I flop on the couch and flip open my laptop after Caleb goes to work. This was the first time in ages that I felt relaxed enough to let Caleb reciprocate. And I enjoyed it…a lot. So, I'm equipped to handle whatever my first stop, Twitter, throws at me. I have over four-hundred new followers, which might not seem like much, but I only had five hundred to begin with. I'm not exactly Twitter famous. Though looking at these mentions, I might end up that way. *Woman assaulted by Vin Merdone demonstrates the best of humanity in forgiving him* tops a video of me saying, "I forgave you a long time ago…" and my words after, but nothing of my confrontation with him before, my listing of all the things in me he destroyed. Maybe it's better that way. I would rather that moment not go viral. I would rather forget about it, though I'm glad I spoke my truth.

But there's my anger, popping up in another tweet, and another, and another. And then, I notice the hashtags accompanying them: #CancelVinMerdone #CancelMerdone

#NeverMerdone #RefundMerdone, about people getting their donations refunded, and my favorite, #VinMerdone IsOverParty. There are a few slightly different variations of each. Some have only his first name, some his last. But they all say the same thing, and it couldn't make me happier. Even Trump tweeted about him, *Stone cold looser CryVin Merdone cries when his victim yells at him. Violent guy. Bad News. Heard People say He's like Trump. No way.* Ugh, he can't even spell "loser." I think Vin would have actually been better than Trump. What have I done?

My phone chimes with a text from Sean, and I scroll right past him to my sisters' texts. Jamie texted me a line of crying emojis and *I'm proud of you little sis.* Laura texted me, *Way to go. You told him. I'm sorry I didn't know. I was so busy chasing after toddlers when you were in college, sorry I wasn't there for you.* I thank them both and text each an avi of me blowing a heart kiss to let them know how much I appreciate it. Though, it rings a bit hollow since I didn't answer until the next day. I text *I'm sorry* to both of them.

Sean's text says, *Did you see #CancelMerdone is trending? I'm so proud of you. Love you, babe. You did this. You're a rock star. I bet he drops out any minute.*

I put the phone down. I wonder what Nicole would think if she saw that text. I go back on my phone and delete it because I know what Caleb would think. I haven't even seen Nicole in years. She was with Sean when I ran into him at the supermarket once. I had never met her before, but since I had been stalking his Facebook at the time, I knew what she looked like. Though under the harsh fluorescent lights in the store she looked much older than the photos—in fact, she looked much older than Sean, who still had a baby face in his late thirties. I remembered their age difference as soon she leaned in and shook my hand. She was still beautiful to be sure, but the fake smile plastered on her face and her icy demeanor before walking away, made her less so.

Looking back now, though, I feel bad for Nicole. I always thought of her as the enemy. She was the one who tore me and Sean apart, but it wasn't her fault. I was the one who took too long to let Sean know how I felt. And now when I think about how I could have been the one to marry Sean if I had told him I loved him, I realize that fate, or my paralysis, worked in my favor. I could never have predicted Trump, and I could never have predicted that he would drive a wedge between me and Sean. And it's about so much more than politics.

I knew Sean was a Republican way back—I didn't care. I respected his political views, as he did mine. But, while I would have been more than happy to continue our friendship, albeit not quite as close, if Sean hadn't lied to me about Gina, I don't know if I'd be able to be married to someone who so staunchly supports everything that is the antithesis of what I believe. I don't know if I'd be able to be married to someone who would lie just to protect those beliefs. So, I think I dodged a bullet, or I may have been filing for divorce papers.

It feels a bit harsh to me to even think that I would divorce Sean over his political views—and maybe it's colored by the fact that he lied to me—but, I suddenly feel more grateful for Caleb than I ever have. Yes, we have had our ups and downs, and he lied to me about his porn habit, but he apologized and didn't lie to me on the same scale that Sean did.

I'm curious if I'm right about how hard it would be to be married to Sean as a liberal, so I Google *Trump supporter and non-supporter divorce*. Immediately, several articles pop up. *Trump Presidency is Destroying Marriages Across the Country*, a *Daily News* article from 2017 catches my eye immediately. I was not wrong to think that Sean and I may have ended up divorced. I think I can be friends with him again, when the sting of what he did subsides, but it's a relief to feel that everything that happened between us happened for a reason.

Next, I check my Facebook notifications, and I'm immediately overwhelmed. I usually try to answer, or at least like, every mention or comment on my posts. I'm nothing if not polite. But I have no hope of doing that. Rolling Green Resists alone probably has twenty-five mentions. I read a few of them, but I don't want to answer some and not all, so I post in the group that I'm grateful for all the support and will read all the messages when I can. The ones I read are all positive—*You rock. Vin will never get my vote!*—and the like. I'm deeply grateful for my friends, some of whom I've never met in real life, even though we live in the same town. We sometimes have post-card writing parties for Democratic candidates, even in "off" years when local elections make up the ballot, but not everyone in the group makes it. We all know local elections impact your life on a day to day basis and work to get our candidates elected. We bond, we laugh, and we eat lots of snacks.

After being in residential, I swore that I would try new things when my kids got old enough, and I had some time on my hands. Getting involved in local politics seemed natural after Trump was elected, but I worked behind the scenes. Reading some more of the posts, though, I start wondering if maybe I should come out from behind the scenes. More than one person suggested that I run for Town Council. *Maybe someday*, I type on one post. I add *Thank you* with a smiley kiss emoji. "Maybe someday," I repeat aloud and smile.

There's one more thing I need to do on my laptop before I get off my ass and do laundry. I click on the town shelter's website and on one of the thumbnails, a pit bull with a haunted look in her eyes and a brow wrinkled with worry.

Her stomach hangs low, teats practically dragging on the ground—she's a throwaway mama. I saw her earlier on Facebook and recognized that look of trauma because, to be honest, I've had it myself. But I also recognized it because our dog, Rose, had it and I miss her so very much still.

Seeing Emily, I know that I'm finally ready to adopt again. The listing said she was named for Emily Dickinson, this region's favorite daughter. Her bio said, "Emily dwells in possibility...the possibility that she'll know love, happiness and a home of her own," a play on an Emily Dickinson quote. I text her photo to Caleb with the message, *Let's celebrate. I'm ready.*

His response is an immediate *Yes!!!*

He's wanted another dog for a while. I was the one who was trying to get over the heartbreak of losing our first dog. But I feel ready now, and I think rescuing a dog will distract me and let me focus on something bigger than my issues. I'm saving a life.

Caleb comes home at lunchtime, so we can go to the shelter together. And of course, it's instant love. Emily is shaking in the back of her cage, her big body and meatball head seemingly shrunken—she's crouched down as small as she can get. I kneel down as the shelter worker brings her out of her cage and let her sniff my hand. One sniff...then a tentative lick, and very slowly I move my hand up and scratch behind her ears. Suddenly, her marbled brownie body is leaning into me. It's a full-on, future Velcro dog lean, and my heart is hers.

I turn to Caleb, "Well?"

He kneels down and calls Emily to him; she warily approaches and sniffs his hand. "Hey sweetie, do you want to come home with us?" He kisses the top of her chunk head, and I fall in love with him all over again. Emily looks up adoringly at Caleb and kisses his face.

I turn to the shelter worker and say, "We want her—what do we need to do?"

She smiles broadly and motions to the door leading back into the main area. It kills me to leave the other dogs, all of whom are either whining or barking, but at least I know that it's a no-kill shelter. "You just need to fill out the paperwork. She's already spayed and has her shots. You can take her right home."

"No home visit or anything?"

"Unfortunately, or maybe fortunately for you, since it's quicker, we don't do those as a town shelter. Private rescues will always do that. We just don't have the resources. But to be honest, I have my own gut instincts, and I can tell that you'll give Emily a great home."

"You hear that, Emily? We're going to give you a great home."

We stop at Target on the way home to buy a bed, toys, food and a pale pink, fluffy doggie sweater. Because she's so underweight and because her fur is still so patchy—completely absent in spots—the shelter suggested she wear a sweater outside until the New England chill gives way to warmer days.

Bringing Emily home accomplishes exactly what I hoped, in addition to saving her life, of course...I haven't looked at my phone all day, and it's almost 6:00 p.m. I always tell the boys if they need me, and I don't answer a text to call the house phone, so I know they're okay. My mom only calls my house phone, so I know I haven't missed anything from her either. It's kind of liberating not checking it every ten minutes.

Jacob and Oliver will be home any minute, so I take Emily upstairs and put her in my room so I can surprise them. I bring up her bed, the little dog blanket and a super soft squirrel toy we got her. I tuck her in and give her a treat before I head back downstairs to make dinner and wait for the boys. I pop some hot dogs in the oven to broil and empty a can of baked beans into a microwave bowl—fastest meal I can think of—then run back up to check on Emily and bring her a bowl of water.

The boys come barreling in as I come down the stairs. They smell like fresh grass and sweat from baseball practice (which is a surprisingly *not* unpleasant scent—maybe because it brings me back to when they were in Little League). I tell them, "I have a surprise for you guys, but you have to wait for Dad to come home. I'll check and see where he is." Since I don't want to call if he's in a meeting, I grab my phone from where it's been charging to check his location.

I very quickly scroll through my texts and see one from Vin, asking to meet with me, right below one from Sean asking if I'm okay. I take a deep breath and I put the phone down. I am not going to let him ruin this moment. I've had anxiety invade so many special moments in my family's life. This will not be one of them. I don't need to see him; I don't even need to answer the text. I definitely do not need to ponder the reasons he may want to see me. I can assume it's because his campaign is on the rocks, and he wants me to make a statement or something exonerating him. Never. I call Caleb from the house phone instead. He should be out of his meetings anyway. "Almost home?" I ask quickly when he answers.

"Yup. Two minutes."

"Okay, because our surprise is waiting, and I don't want to leave it too long."

The boys look confused. Jacob speaks first, "Did you buy us presents or something? Ooh…did you get me a car?'

"She said a surprise for *us*, Dipwad," Oliver chimes in. "Plus, how would she hide a freakin' car?"

"Oliver!"

"Sorry. Okay, what is it? I'm hungry. And I want to get on Xbox. My friends are waiting for me."

"You need to do your homework first. Plus, when you see the surprise, Xbox won't seem that exciting. I made hot dogs and baked beans for dinner. They just need to cook for a few minutes."

"Beans, beans, the musical fruit…the more you eat, the more you toot," Oliver sings and for just a moment, I can see the little boy he was before stretching out into an almost man. He'll be taller than Jacob for sure. He's already just about 5'10" and will still grow at least a couple more inches.

"Honey, I'm hooome," Caleb calls out in his best Ricky Ricardo voice, and I literally jump up and down excitedly. I run upstairs and pick up Emily. I know once she gains weight and fills out, I won't be able to do this. She's a "pocket pittie," but she'll still be about fifty pounds. Right now, she's not much more than thirty or thirty-five if that. It's like lifting a preschooler. Still, carrying a wiggly dog down the steep steps of our old house seems a bit of a dangerous proposal, so I put her down and guide her down the stairs by pulling a treat out of my pocket and walking just ahead of her.

When we walk in the kitchen, my teenage stoics melt into little boys again, and I love it. They both crouch down and shower Emily with kisses and hugs. She clearly loves the attention, returning the kisses, bathing their faces. Oliver looks up, a huge smile on his face, "Holy crap! You got another dog! What's her name? When? How?"

I plop down on the floor next to them, and Emily maneuvers onto my lap, clearly thinking she weighs twenty pounds less than she does, but I don't mind. "Dad and I adopted her today from the shelter. Her name is Emily for Emily Dickinson. I guess we can change it, if you want, but I kind of like it."

"She's so cute, it doesn't matter what her name is," Jacob practically gushes, and I love it.

"Emily it is, then. And as for how…well, I just saw her photo this morning, and she reminded me of Rose—the look in her eyes, and I kind of feel like she sent her to us, crazy as that may seem." I mean Rose our dog, but to be honest, her haunted look reminded me a little of Rose the person, too. And it reminded me that I made a promise to myself to keep living, to keep moving forward, to honor her memory always. Doing something normal and joyous, like adopting Emily, takes the focus off of my anxiety over Vin and everything that has happened. It's keeping me moving forward, not looking back.

Caleb sits down next to me and scratches behind Emily's ears. She leans one way and then the other. She scooches just a bit forward halfway off my lap and kisses him, then looks up and kisses me under my chin. The oven beeps, so I ask, "Who wants her next? The hot dogs are ready."

Both boys reach for Emily, and she settles in between them as one rubs her belly and one scratches behind her ears. I stand up and just gaze at the scene before turning to take out the hot dogs before they burn. I pull the bowl of baked beans I cooked before the boys got home out of the microwave and plate everything. I break off a piece of hot dog and toss it to Emily. She gobbles it up. I have to admit, though I rarely make hot dogs, I made them tonight with Emily in mind. I grab my plate and sit down, not daring to even glance at my phone.

*   *   *

After I tuck Emily into her dog bed with her soft blanket, I exhaustedly fall into bed and turn to Caleb. "Cal, do you realize that this is the first time in ages that the boys didn't escape into their rooms right after dinner?"

"I do. I think Miss Emily worked her magic on them. Thank you, Miss Emily," he calls to her and she looks up at him adoringly. It takes only a second before she's out of her bed and scratching on ours, crying plaintively.

"I know we shouldn't," I say.

"You're absolutely right," Caleb agrees.

One more cry, and I'm out of the bed and picking Emily up. She snuggles between us, and both of us are pushed to our respective edges of the mattress. "You didn't want any action tonight, did you?" I ask Caleb.

"What is it, my birthday? After the action I got this morning, I don't expect anything else today—tomorrow maybe, but not today," Caleb chuckles and winks at me. "Seriously, though is your jaw sore?"

"Nope, I'm good," I answer, and I mean it as I snuggle in with Emily and drift off into an easy sleep.

6:30 a.m. comes way too quickly, and I don't even look at my phone when my alarm goes off, I just hit the screen with my eyes closed until the jarring tone is silenced. I have no idea if I've hit snooze or turned it off, so I have to pick it up and turn my alarm again. That's when I'm reminded that I haven't gone on it since yesterday, and I have texts waiting from Vin and Sean. I can't ignore them forever, and now I'm wide awake. So, I get up and head into the boys' rooms to wake them, Emily trailing behind me.

First, we wake Oliver, and it hasn't been this easy since he started high school. Emily jumps on him and kisses his face, and he's awake in a second. We repeat it with Jacob. They both whine a little about leaving her but are out the door before Caleb is even awake. I make myself a cup of tea and sit down to read Vin and Sean's texts. I don't have much of an appetite for breakfast yet and frankly, it's a bit scary. So, I pat the couch next to me for Emily to jump up. I hold her for a bit and then tackle my texts when my heart slows down.

I read Vin's first, *Kate, can we meet tomorrow? I'm still in town and I'd like for you to be a part of my campaign moving forward. Of course, I'd pay you generously. I can use your insight and marketing skills. And you seem pretty popular here. Seeing the way the crowd reacted to you last night I knew I wanted to somehow harness that enthusiasm. You were amazing and articulate. So, I checked your LinkedIn and was very impressed. So lucky that you're in marketing. And to be honest, your speech has lost me some momentum, so hoping you can help me turn it around. You know how bad I feel about what I did.*

I write back one word: *No.* Such a small, but powerful word. And that word had no power twenty-six years ago when Vin had me pinned to the bed, but now...now I believe it has all the power I need. That text was so out of bounds—clearly written by someone who is used to getting what he wants. I don't care if he complimented me, it was still narcissistic of him to assume I would want to work with him, to assume I would even want to be in the same room with him ever again.

It is hard for me to not send a follow-up *Sorry* text. I'm used to apologizing when I say, "No." If I can't help someone for any reason, I always feel like I owe an apology. But I remind myself that I owe Vin nothing. I move onto Sean's texts. The first one just asks, *Are you still mad at me?* The next is longer: *We have been friends for almost thirty years. Are you going to throw that away over political differences? I know I lied and I'm sorry. But I swear that my biggest reason for doing what I did was to get you to confront Vin and finally get rid of your demons. You have to believe me. And it helped, right? Trump is not more important than us. I don't love him—I just like some of what he does. I'm not one of those drinking the Kool Aid people and if someone better comes along, I'll vote for that person. But Vin wasn't it.*

The third text just says, *OK. I get it. You don't want to talk to me. I even tried calling, but no answer. I didn't leave a VM. I won't bother you anymore. I'm sorry. That's really all I can say.*

Oh, and I like Pete Buttigieg. I think I would vote for him over Trump. I don't like any of the other candidates, but I like him. You see—I'm open to other candidates.

I don't think I can stay mad at Sean, as much as I'm not quite ready to let this righteous indignation go. He lied to me. Caleb hates him. He forgave Trump's most egregious sins. I have every reason to cut him out of my life. But he's still my friend, and I still care about him. I have to find a way to look past all the turbulence that has tossed our relationship about. I have missed him these past few years, even as Caleb and I have grown stronger, and I need Sean less. He's no longer a crutch, which is a good thing.

Before I can answer Sean's text, a text from Vin pops up. *Anything I can do to get you to reconsider? Did I mention I pay very well? And you can make your own hours and mostly work from home.*

There's no amount of money that could persuade me to work for Vin—maybe a million dollars, so we could buy a bigger house, and I can pay for my kids' college, but nothing he would realistically pay me. I get on Twitter before I answer him. I want to see what the collateral damage of my rally appearance is.

Looking at Twitter, I know why he's so desperate. *#CancelMerdone* is still trending, along with *#NeverMerdone* and *#MerdoneIsOverParty*. For a brief second I feel bad for him, but only for a brief second. This couldn't have happened to a better guy. He deserves every bit of scorn. And he should consider himself lucky—considering what he did to me and likely to other women, he could have spent years rotting in jail. He's a multi-millionaire, and this was probably a vanity run anyway.

Thankfully, people are wising up to the fact that we don't need another millionaire nor billionaire outsider/sexual predator. Yes, Vin apologized for his actions, and I forgave him. But that doesn't erase what he did. That doesn't suddenly make him a good person. Just like everything that Sean has done doesn't make him a bad person. There's a lot of gray in each of us. Caleb and I learned that the hard way five years ago. His porn habit and my emotional affair were twin thorns in the side of our marriage, and I'm forever grateful that we overcame them.

I text back Sean before I answer Vin. *I didn't look at my phone all day because we adopted a new dog. Her name is Emily. She's a very good girl. And she's already helped distract me from my anxieties. My phone fuels my anxiety right now, so I stayed off it all day yesterday. Emily arriving home made it easy. Look, I'll get there with you. We have a history. I can't just ignore that. We've never agreed on politics, but I always respected your views. You know that. But Trump is more than politics. When you support him, it feels to me like you support predators, racists, and everything else horrible that he stands for. I can compartmentalize in my relationships—I didn't unfriend anyone because of Trump, I could still see the value in my relationships with my friends and family who support him. And believe me, I know you're more than your political views, but when those views are so damaging to my psyche, it hurts. That's why while I'll never end a relationship with you or anyone else based solely on Trump, there are times I've needed to step back. I hope you understand that. Thanks for saying you'd be willing to support a Dem. Now the lying is a bit harder to get over. But I want to forgive you. I really do. I want to forget. I'm going to choose to believe that you were acting in my best interests, but if I ever find out that you lied to me about that, I will not forgive you. Understand?* I can't get over the expanse of blue that pops up on my screen when I send the text—it's longer than it seemed when I was typing.

Still, Sean's answer is almost immediate, *Of course I understand. Thank you for giving me a second chance. You were always one of my best friends and time and the wounds we inflicted on each other over the years won't change that. For a* moment I wonder if he could have possibly read the whole message, but then I decide that it doesn't matter. Even if he skimmed it, he got the idea.

Thanks. So—reset? That's what we would say whenever we argued when we were in college. We didn't fight a lot, but we had some disagreements here and there—stupid things. And we'd just say, "Reset," and we could move on. There were many times I wish I had said it at the bar on that night so long ago before I stormed away from him. But I guess it all worked out the way it was supposed to.

Reset with a kiss emoji pops up on my home screen. I send a thumbs-up and click on Vin's text.

I type quickly. *No. There's nothing you can do to make me reconsider. Please don't ask me again. Thank you. You never suffered any consequences for what you did, while I've been paying for decades. I nearly paid with my life. So no, I can't help you get elected. And I don't need the money that badly. Good luck to you.* I hit send before I can change it to sound nicer. It is exquisitely uncomfortable for me not to say, "I appreciate the offer" or "I'm sorry." But Vin deserves neither. Even the "Good luck" is more than he deserves. The "Thank you" is more than he deserves. So, I quickly text, *I can forgive, but I'll never forget, motherfucker.*

I pull Emily back to me, and she gladly snuggles in, putting her head on my lap and kissing my hand as I scratch under her chin. Dog therapy is the best, and I'm awash with gratitude that I found little Miss Emily on Facebook at exactly the moment I needed her. I don't know who rescued whom. I felt the same with our first dog, Rose.

My phone lights up next to me with a message from Vin. It simply says, *I'm sorry* with three crying emojis following. "You should be," I say out loud. "Come on, Em. Let's have some breakfast. "You want some scrambled eggs with me?" Emily's wiggle butt is in overdrive as she follows me into the kitchen. She's at my feet as I cook the eggs, adding in milk and a little maple syrup as I whisk them into a fluffy froth.

When they're done, and I've buttered two pieces of toast, I give Emily a few pieces of egg in her bowl and sit at the kitchen table with my mug of tea and a magazine. I eat slowly, piling the eggs on my golden, glistening toast triangles and savoring each bite. My anxiety is gone...at least for right now. And I know enough to appreciate how special this moment really is.

EPILOGUE

September 2019

I DON'T KNOW if I delivered the fatal blow to Vin's campaign when I appeared at his rally or when I refused to join it, but amidst lots of pushback from women's groups, people who just don't like predators and of course DNC operatives, Vin ended his campaign a lot more quietly than he started it. By late-May he was polling at below one percent and the second week in June, even before the first debate, he announced that he was "indefinitely suspending" his campaign, which everyone knew meant he was dropping out. Once a campaign is suspended, it's not coming back. I couldn't be happier.

If Trump wins again, I might question whether maybe I should have put the country over my own vendetta for revenge. But boy, does it feel good right now. I know I always fantasized about plunging a knife into Vin's heart, but I knew I would never do that. And plunging a metaphorical knife into his campaign felt even better than any homicidal fantasy. I still wish he spent time in jail, but at least he failed spectacularly and faced the wrath of many.

Vin even lost control of his own company when he was ousted by the board of directors after a few more women from his past rose up and told their stories. Each woman recounted a story from college or just after. There were three in all, plus his ex-girlfriend from that time whom he punched. None were within the last quarter of a century, and I do believe that Vin turned his life around when he got sober. But actions have consequences—even actions taken as a young man. And I'm glad he's living them now. Better late than never. And his campaign did do some good, like his donation to RAINN. When he suspended his campaign he promised to continue to work tirelessly to right all the wrongs he committed in the past, tweeting, *I'll put my money where my mouth is and continue to donate to causes that lift up women and help survivors of violence.* I hope he does. It may be the one redeeming thing he can do.

Vin's fall from grace was swift, but my ascension has been even quicker. I've discovered my calling, and it's working to effect change right here in my little college town. After much prompting from the ladies in Rolling Green Resists, I declared my candidacy for mayor in August. Even though Rolling Green is liberal, we've had a Republican mayor for almost two decades. He's been in office since 2000—he's from one of the oldest families in Rolling Green and just keeps getting voted back into office, even while the Town Council has leaned Democratic for at least a dozen years. His father held the seat before he did, so he has history on his side. And he's on the board of the college, as well as being one of its biggest benefactors.

He made a misstep though that galvanized Rolling Green Resists and the town as a whole. He vetoed a measure requiring that all educational institutions in the town, including Rolling Green College, must report all sexual assaults to the town police, not just campus police, or worse, just refer the perpetrator to the academic judiciary process, where a mere slap on the wrist was likely, especially if a parent is a donor to the school. The Town Council was furious that their five – two vote was reversed. The two council members who voted against the measure were the mayor's brother and cousin. In order to overcome the veto, at least one of them would have had to change his vote. That didn't happen.

There was much discussion in our Rolling Green Resists Facebook group about what we could do to fight back. I suggested that one of us should run for mayor...and it was unanimous that I should be the one to do it. It made perfect sense. I've lived in the town for all but one year of the past twenty-seven. I planned tons of events which required me to work with all sorts of municipal services. And after my appearance at Vin's rally, I became somewhat of a local celebrity, at least to the women in town. I have to admit, it would be a pretty sweet reckoning for someone who enables rape culture to be beaten by me, a survivor.

It's been a ton of work already, even though I'm just getting started, and I'm over a year out from the election in November 2020. I've rented a storefront in town that had been vacant for ages with a lawyer who's running for state senate, Elaine Smith. She and I have made it our joint campaign headquarters. This way we can share resources and double our power in reaching out to the electorate. Admittedly, her campaign is more expansive and complicated, since it's for state government, rather than town, so I help her out with research and designing marketing materials. She gives me free legal advice.

I've fallen into a comfortable rhythm, and I feel enormously grateful, whether I win or lose. If I lose, I'll find some other way to make a difference. And meanwhile, I'm writing my own story each and every day. I get to have Emily snoozing at my feet while I work. And Caleb and I have lunch together most days, since his office is around the corner. In fact, he should be walking in the door any minute.

We eat at the pizza and pasta joint; the sandwich shop; the coffee bar for a quick snack; even the fancy bistro once in a while. And none of it scares me. I dash out for frozen yogurt in the late afternoon and always spoon a generous amount of peanut butter cups on top. I've even gained a few pounds since I've been in this routine, but Caleb loves my curves. And I've started lifting weights three nights a week, so I'm stronger every day. I know Jacob and Oliver are proud of me, they tell me all the time now…and that's the most important thing.

Sean and I have continued our détente. We don't talk politics at all, although I'd love to hear his take on the almost daily scandals that still swirl around Trump. I'd love to know if he's really okay with his hateful rhetoric. To be honest, I still have a hard time understanding how someone who is so kind can support someone so cruel. I keep thinking that he'll text me and say, *That's it—I'm done with him.* But I don't know if that will ever happen. And I have to be okay with that.

Sean did promise me that he'll vote for me for mayor, even though I'm a Democrat. That means a lot to me, because he's always supported our current mayor, though I imagine he couldn't have been too happy with the veto. When I told him that I intended to run, he texted me, *You have my vote! Sometimes friendships are more important than politics.* I couldn't agree more.

I'm alone in my office when *Don't Give Up*, the song I listened to on my way to the trail, comes up on my playlist. *Don't give up. Don't give up. We all need saving.* Giving up when I've hit rock bottom would have been so much easier than rising up. As I gaze out the big picture window, feeling so grateful that I chose the latter, Caleb walks up to the door. Emily bolts to greet him, and he bends down to scratch behind her ears. She rewards him with a tongue bath all over his face. He takes off his glasses as he stands up and pulls a cloth out of his pocket to wipe off the saliva. "I love you too, Em," he says with a laugh. I rise from my desk to greet him, and he pulls me into a hug. "And I love you, Kate. Have I told you that I'm proud of you?"

"Lots of times. Thank you, babe. Love you more." I go up on my tiptoes to kiss him, and he wraps his arms around me, lifting me off my feet.

"You will no doubt be the sexiest mayor in all of Massachusetts," Caleb practically growls.

I look down at my plain gray cardigan, white tank top and jeans and laugh. "I'm not so sure about that but thank you."

"It's true."

"I have to win first."

"Just remember—in my book you've already won, regardless of whether you become mayor. Every day that you face the world; every day that you eat breakfast, lunch and dinner; every day that you're there for me and the boys…you've won."

"Thank you," is all I can get out. I'm a little choked up. Okay, more than a little. Overcoming an eating disorder isn't really a victory—at least not a total one. It's a journey with victorious stops along the way, but defeat can always be around the next corner. Any victory is temporary. Here's the thing, though—the more years that stretch out between those defeats, the more likely, and long lasting, the victories. And right now, I'm smack dab in the middle of one of my best victories ever. So, I'm not going to think about what might be looming in the months and years ahead…I'm just going to appreciate the right now.

I give Emily a treat and settle her in her doggy playpen. She's got her cozy bed, fresh water and a peanut butter filled toy to keep her busy. And I've got nothing on my agenda for a couple of hours. I take Caleb by the hand and lead him out into the brilliant late September sunshine. I stop to lock the door and turn back to him. "Let's go eat," I say and relish all that represents.

The End